Praise for NO ONE'S LEAVING

Raki Kopernik's debut novel, *No One's Leaving*, is a grief narrative unlike any other I've read. It manages to be devastatingly painful, haunted with heartache, and also sidesplittingly funny, full of kindness, queerness, and warmth. Gritty and honest as a Patti Smith song, No One's Leaving is a story about travel, about the love of strangers, about letting go and starting again. Kopernik's keen insights on love and loss are profound. Each line, sharp and true.

-Alissa Hattman, author of *Sift*

No One's Leaving exists in the liminal spaces between life and death, truth and fiction, pain and healing. Throughout the narrator's fevered journey across Europe and the US after the suicide of her ex, we become unable to separate ourselves from her so that her meditations, her hauntings, her travels become our own. Confessional, raw, and poetic, this is a novel that dazzles the reader from a writer exercising her full power.

-Darci Schummer, author of *Six Months in the Midwest*

Ethereal and atmospheric, Kopernik's prose seamlessly weaves together the memories of a haunting love and a present unraveling adventure. As the narrator embarks on a journey to heal from the past, she contemplates loss—all its pain and suffering—and finds an opportunity for introspection, deep reflection and meditation. *No One's Leaving* is a fever dream of grief, an eloquent song of trauma and rebirth.

-Brittany Ackerman, author of *The Perpetual Motion Machine* and *The Brittanys*

Full of portals to the past and passageways forward, *No One's Leaving* is an underground-guidebook-cum-queer-odyssey traversing loss and the many I's grief sheds. Charting a journey from hostels to ferries to farmfields to yurts to hitched rides, Raki Kopernik's crisp and clear storytelling is charmed and generous, like the eyes of love, showing us how to trust ourselves, how to move through blue, how to surrender and sync with the rhythm of the living even when haunted by the dead, and how to start, again and again and again.

-Elisabeth Workman, author of *Ultramegaprairieland* and *Endlessness Is No Desolation*

No One's Leaving

Raki Kopernik

They may say, those were the days… But in a way/ You know
for us these are the days. Yes, for us these are the days.

-Jane's Addiction

For Val, RIP

PART ONE

1.

THE PLANE LANDED in Paris and I was alone. I took a train to Amsterdam without smelling a moment of French air. Paris was not the beginning. Holland waterways and families on bicycles, five people two pedals, babies to grans all together, was the beginning. Cafés with tiny cups of coffee and huge joints for sale served by faux redheaded punky girls, was the beginning. Everything is tidier when you leave America. Even mess.

I didn't cry until I got to Amsterdam. I was leaning on the metal railing of a bridge overlooking the Zwanenburgwal canal. My chest cracked, my eyes filled. I leaned forward, pressing my guts into the railing. Water dumped out into the canal in giant plops. I watched the puddles make loops, sound waves expanding out and out and out, interlacing each other, syncopating. One drop, ten drops, twenty drops of water don't make a difference in volume, but every drop changes the chemistry. When my eyes ran out of water, I looked at the wavy mirror of my face against the canal. My brown eyes turned blue in its reflection. Her blue.

Her eyes in my eyes in the waters of Amsterdam.

I see you, I said.

Her laugh, her shadows, her death not death.

Are you following me? I said out loud.

A boat passed through the canal and her blue eyes turned to waves then to nothing. People passing by in the boat waved up, shouting and laughing. I waved back, searching for her face in the crowd.

2.

The trip was planned long before her dust was watered into the base of a Virginia oak. I was on the East coast, not far from where she hung. Her sister picked me up in a silver Subaru. We drove six hours from Brooklyn to Virginia. We had never met.

She called you the fancy sister, I said.

I didn't know that, she said. Her eyes red and full of water.

I looked out the window at the fresh budding trees and stayed quiet for the rest of the ride. When we arrived, people were drinking wine out of hand-made ceramic mugs in Earth tone colors. I didn't know anyone and I had never been to Virginia. I stood on a wooden deck overlooking an oak-pine forest.

My dad built this house when we were kids, the sister said.

She told me that, I said.

He found her hanging under the deck, she said.

I looked down at my feet.

Right underneath us, she said, looking down too.

I pictured her dad sitting in his rocking chair, rocking, then stopping and still hearing the rocking. I pictured him following the sound until he found its source. I pictured his face turning white like hers probably was and trying to cut the rope around her throat. I didn't cry. But I wanted to throw up.

You can sleep in her room. Go through her closet and take whatever you want, her dad said.

I felt his eyes trying to connect to mine. I looked at him for a second, then walked to the closet.

I'll leave you be, he said. He closed the door.

I opened it back up halfway and watched his bedroom door close behind him down the hall. Candles were still lit throughout the house, and they made moving shadows on the ceiling.

Ghosts of my memories.

Everything woven in invisible fishing twine, strong and see-through.

In the olden days, when candles and oil were the only sources of light, everyone looked beautiful like transparent sepia spirits.

I found the collared gray shirt in her closet. The one I always borrowed when I needed something sort-of fancy. Its faint silver stripes shimmered in the right light and showed my clavicles just enough. It looked good on her, and I wanted to look like her. The shirt looked small and empty hanging from a plastic hanger amongst clothes I had never seen. I wanted to take everything. I put the shirt on the bed and lay next to it on top of the covers. I listened to my breath, in out up down, and noticed a faint smell of sage and chocolate. My eyes were heavy and my heart felt tired. I closed my eyes, but they wouldn't stay closed even though it was hard to keep them open.

Not one, not the other.

The beginning, the end, and the middle.

I didn't sleep, but time passed and rooms became dark. A memory of her face, the sound of her laughing, that time we kissed on the futon of our apartment. That time I loved her. I opened the door. All the candles had been blown out but their shadows were still cast, moving along the ceiling. I sat on the hallway rug and looked up. Her shadow laughing through old wooden boards of this cabin her father built. I heard the high pitch of her otherwise alto voice, how it rose only when she laughed. Distinctly her.

I'm not mad at you, I said.

In the morning, I drank the black coffee they made, took the chocolate they offered, and after sitting around an oak tree listening to stories I had never heard, the sister took me to the train station. We hugged and I felt guilty for the fancy sister comment. She was thin and sad and looked as though words could crack her skin and crumble her bones.

I rode the train back to New York to get on a plane to Europe and start an adventure I wasn't sure I still wanted to have. But it felt too late to turn back, and too boring not to move forward.

3.

As the day progressed, I walked through the cobblestone streets of Holland without focus, my feet guiding my body, my body floating along. I found myself in a grocery store where I bought a cucumber and a baguette and made my way to a nearby park bench. A young German raver guy in baggy pants sat next to me and smiled. He lit up a joint and offered it to me.

Danke, I said. The only German I knew. He nodded his head and smiled bigger. I ripped off a piece of my baguette and gave it to him.

Tonk you, he said. The only English he knew.

He looked up and pointed at the tree above us. Two small blue and orange Kingfishers were sharing a worm. We watched the birds for the duration of the joint and after. We couldn't stop watching them.

The blue of the birds, the blue of her eyes, crisp and clear.

I have never seen eyes like hers. Maybe her eyes let in too much light. No pigment, no filter. Some people see too much, feel everything too much. Maybe that's the wrong way to look at it. Maybe it's not too much, but so much. More than my own tank has the capacity for.

I looked back at the German and he looked at me. He was smiling, his lids half closed, stoned. He glowed with a pink light like what I imagine an aura would be. I smiled back at him and he started to say something I didn't understand. At my confused expression, he ran a finger down his cheek like a tear and pointed at me. I put my hands on my chest. He touched my shoulder. We took a deep breath together, then finished the baguette and looked back up at the birds.

That night, I slept in a dirty hostel in the middle of the city in a room full of bunk beds with itchy blankets. I didn't remember any of my dreams. It was a hard, long sleep, the kind that feels like nothing, like you close your eyes and open them a minute later and it's the next day. My eyes opened. I drank a tiny cup of coffee in the hostel café and walked to the train station to find the next new beginning.

4.

When the train doors closed, I felt safe. There's nothing to figure out when everything is moving. Stillness is coveted, and so arduous to accept. I sat down next to a young blond guy with blond eyelashes wearing a white shirt, bright like the high noon sun. I handed the conductor my ticket.

Bruges, I said.

You have a good accent, the conductor said.

I also speak Hebrew, I said.

He smiled and punched my ticket and the blond-haired blond-eyelash guy next to me said, Gam ani medaber ivrit.

I asked him where he was from and how he knew Hebrew.

Russia via Poland but now living in Israel. I'm traveling through Europe trying to figure out where to live next. I just broke up with my boyfriend. My name is Konrad, he said in Hebrew.

We shook hands and fell in friend love.

Konrad was tall and beautiful with a big nose and sleepy eyes under all the blond. The more he talked the gayer he became, the more I knew I had made the right choice to go to Belgium. Keep moving, stay free.

I'm going to Bruges too, he said. Let's share a room.

Bruges looked like a BBC period piece, cobblestone streets, old brick buildings with verandas and chocolate shops that served tiny pieces of chocolate and espresso in even tinier cups. Everywhere I went I had tiny coffee. Konrad wanted to stay in a fancy hotel with white sheets and eat fancy spaghetti with white napkins. I splurged, happy to have a friend and a clean bed for the first time in a week. We walked around the quiet town, posing in front of old pointy churches and sluggish canals to take pictures with each other's cameras.

My father died in a factory machine accident in Poland when I was ten, Konrad said between bites of spaghetti. We were broken, just like Poland was. I always knew I was gay. But being gay over there was death. I still won't go back, he said.

I always think of Poland as shtetls and babushkas, I said.

That's about right, he said.

My ex-girlfriend just died, I said.

People can die so easily, he said. He took a gulp of thick red wine.

Well, she died on purpose, I said.

It's hard to stay alive, he said.

I see her everywhere.

Do you see her now?

I usually see her when I'm alone.

I never saw my father again after he died.

He has probably seen you, I said.

I had a dream, or maybe I was awake, that my body lifted up and out into the Belgian sky, a constellation of stars changing each time I exhaled, looked away, then looked back. Like Christmas lights syncopating on and off, floating, scattered rhythms, jazz with a beat. I was flying and I knew I could fly. There was no fear, but also, no ground. Like being on a roller coaster in that moment you come out from being upside down. It's so scary, but not if you trust that you are held. Trust is the magic that turns fear into love and adventure.

Go to Ireland, she said.

I'm going to Ireland, I said to Konrad the next morning over more tiny coffee.

I had a feeling you were ready to go somewhere new, he said. I'm going to Italy. I'll take you to the train station.

Konrad helped me find the train to Ostend, a coastal Belgian town, where I could get on a boat to Dover, England, cross England by train, then get on another boat to Ireland.

Wait here I'll be right back, he said.

I stood near the train terminal with my backpack and a package of dark Belgian chocolate. Konrad returned holding a bouquet of red and white daisies. He looked into my eyes and handed me the bouquet.

If only you were a boy, he said.

If only you were a girl, I said.

We laughed together and hugged like old friends. I got on the train smiling, smelling my flowers, and watched him walk away.

5.

She was standing in the corner of the train, staring at me through her black-rimmed glasses, smoking. Her blue eyes reflecting rings of smoke, dulling their color. I wasn't surprised to see her, but I wasn't calm either.

You can't smoke on the train, I said.

We were alone in the train car. She smiled. She was smoking a Virginia Slim, which we called vagina slimes, and only smoked because her mom smoked them when we were in high school. She lived with her mom and sisters in a two-bedroom apartment a few blocks from my house. A classic brick four-plex full of cats and strangers coming and going. Her mom worked long hours on the weekends and late at night as a waitress at a diner, plenty of time to scan the ashtrays around the apartment for half smoked cigarette butts. When her mom was too tired to go to the corner store down the street, she'd send her daughters with a note and two dollars for a pack of Virginia Slims. A note with her mom's signature was all they needed to sell cigarettes to minors. Sometimes we forged the signature. Or we bought cigarettes from one of the machines around town, the ones with big knobs attached to levers you pulled out, causing the pack to drop to the bottom with a thud, like a soda machine. There was one at the ice-skating rink, and one at the restaurant where her mom worked. Her mom caught her oldest sister smoking in the apartment when she was fourteen. They sat down at the kitchen table, mother and daughter face to face, with a fresh pack of cigarettes.

If you can smoke them all, you can smoke all you like, her mom said.

Her sister sucked down one cigarette after the next until she finished the pack, hardly a cough along the way. She filled an amber glass ashtray, like the ones in shabby restaurants with three evenly spaced divots to rest your cigarette. The ashtray got so full of speckled beige butts they had to use a saucer for the last few. Her first and middle fingers turned piss yellow and the house, my friend remembered, was so smoky she couldn't see the dyed red hair on her mother's head. Her mother's laugh was full of smoke, crusty like she might start coughing at the end, which she often did. After that, mother and daughter smoked together daily.

I told her she couldn't smoke on the train, but I wanted her cigarette. I wanted the smoke coming out of her mouth to blow directly in mine. I moved toward her. She relaxed as I approached, lighting another cigarette with the one she was smoking, extending it out toward me. That was how we did it, cherry to cherry. I reached two fingers out. My hand felt hot. Her laugh Dolby surround sound. I pulled on the cigarette, bitter yellow smoke filling the cavity of my mouth. I felt my teeth stain immediately. My gums ached. My lungs cringed. It was disgusting.

I wanted it and I hated it.

I coughed and blew a forceful puff of dirty gray air into her face.

When the smoke cleared, she was gone and I was alone again.

6.

The boat ride to Dover was a quick two hours on a speedy boat that induced a sickness in my guts and made my face feel green. A young Scottish guy found me in a corner seat trying to suck air out of a crack in the window. He asked me something about feeling okay. I told him I could hardly understand his Scottish accent. He said most Scottish people don't even understand each other. I smiled, which he took to mean we were now close. He put his arm around my shoulder and guided me across the aisle to meet his family. Due to my boat illness, I didn't protest. I sat with his family for two hours, nodding at their stories, pretending to understand. When the boat docked, I avoided his eyes and scampered off, hiding in the crowd, into the darkness of night. I found my way to a bed and breakfast around the corner. It was an old house run by a husband and wife with a small child. They all lived downstairs. The husband showed me to my room upstairs.

Hello, I'm Vikrant, he said, extending a hand to shake.

I shook his hand, then he put his hands together at his heart. I did the same. His eyes, black granite that could almost be blue. I looked at his gentle eyes too long and he didn't look away. It's not just about looking people in the eyes, but about the way you look into them.

If you need anything, I will be awake for a few more hours, he said.

His shiny black-blue eyes, full and kind. I nodded.

There is space here for all of your burden, he said.

I didn't say anything, but I thanked him in my mind and I could see in his face that he saw appreciation in my face. Words mean everything and also nothing. You can choose what you say but the feeling behind the sounds decides what the other person receives. He could've said nothing, and I still would've felt all the space he held for me.

Please, he extended his arm toward the room.

The wallpaper was paisley swirls and velvet to the touch, eclectic Victorian. I ran my fingers over the patterns and watched them move around the wall like curling smoke. The swirls moved to make a portrait, the way you can see animals in the clouds, or when your eyes get so relaxed everything is a blur like the Magic Eye books we played with in high school. A repeated pattern of colors and shapes that you press your nose against and pull away slowly to find a three-dimensional picture inside. Objects become other objects, colors become colors that don't exist. Or only exist when you shift yourself enough. I watched the paisley, ran my fingers across the black textures up and down the wall until my arm got too tired to move and my eyelids wilted. In the darkness of eyes closed, her face always arrived and her laugh, always the quiet background soundtrack. Her laugh meant things were okay, we were okay, she was okay. Her laugh was the relief of finally letting the air out after holding it in too long.

Would you like some breakfast? Vikrant asked me the next morning.

I nodded.

His eyes were still warm and smiling. He pulled a chair out for me at a long wooden table next to his wife and baby and handed me a plate of baked beans, sunny side up eggs, and potatoes. I couldn't remember the last time I had baked beans, sweet, tangy, rich, salty. Grounding. I started eating baked beans regularly after that. Although I never liked runny eggs, in that moment, mixed with beans and potatoes and the grace of a baby, nothing felt more like home. Everything is relative to emotions.

You like it? Vikrant's wife asked.

So good thank you, I said with my mouth full.

The baby laughed. Her eyes twinkled, little black diamonds. Babies are intentionally cute so that people will feel overwhelming love for them and care for them. Like animals, they hold secrets without needing words or even sounds. If you look at a baby's eyes and think about love, you can see the glowing thread they extend back to you. The magic of freedom from ego. I looked at the baby and let my heart swell for a moment. She didn't look away.

Vikrant gave me a train schedule and explained the easiest way to walk to the station. I took a picture of his family in my mind and told myself to remember the moment. He put his hands together at his heart again.

Safe travels, safe movement, and enjoy the moments of stillness, he said.

7.

Canterbury is one town over from Dover, one town closer to the other side of England en route to Ireland, a place I have no ancestral connection to, but whose air I have always wanted to breathe in. In my mind, Ireland was a place of enchanted, lush, rolling green hills, the Irish Spring soap commercials of my childhood.

My guidebook pointed me to the cheapest hostel in Canterbury, which turned out to be far from the shitty, thin-mattressed bunk bed hostels I had previously experienced. The place was more like a hotel, soft beds in sturdy frames and bathrooms that looked like they were cleaned regularly. I appreciated the luxury. There was comfort in being in a small, cared for town, like the set of an old British mystery TV show: worn in cobblestone streets, castle shaped buildings made of stone, and small dark pubs on every corner.

Two young Canadian girls were also staying at the hostel, their maple leaf flag patches giving away their identities. They traveled with hair dryers in bulky suitcases and seemed annoyed to have a third in the room we shared. They looked sideways at my dirty, torn jeans and dusty backpack, and I looked at their shiny, blow-dried hair the same way. We didn't talk much, but when we did I pretended to be completely Israeli speaking with my parent's accent, an armor that served me well if not to fool people, to deter them.

On the evening of my arrival, I met Nina. I saw her at the communal dinner table and decided that if she talked to me, I would stay an extra night. Nina had dark, curly hair and sleek green eyes. She was athletic, strong looking and grungy. She looked like my best friend from junior high, Margaret. Margaret was my first crush, that crush you realize only when you're many years removed. She had twelve brothers and sisters. They all played soccer with natural athleticism, like the Partridge Family only sports instead of music. Margaret made me laugh so hard I peed in my pants more than once. We'd get sent out into the hall for laughing, which only gave us more space to laugh. Her house was full of kids kicking soccer balls around inside a living room absent of furniture. Someone was always baking something, someone else always crying, the sounds of life packed so tight into a tiny three-bedroom house I envied. What I envied more was her endless embodied joy, a feeling I thought I could never have if I didn't live in the continual party of her life with her siblings. I visited her house as much as I could, staying as long as I could stand the chaos. The more time I spent with her and grew to know her siblings, the deeper I unknowingly fell for her. I thought about her all the time, as I fell asleep and when I woke in the morning, thinking about funny things to make her laugh. When we laughed together, we looked at each other too long. Her eyes were the first sparkly eyes I never wanted to ever let go of.

I didn't know I really loved Margaret until after she went to the private Catholic girls high school and never spoke to me again. I was leaning into my love for her, and she was learning to shame it away. She broke my heart without knowing. Without her knowing, without my knowing. Maybe her heart was broken too.

Do you like the spaghetti? Nina asked me at dinner.

I nodded.

I made it, she said in a non-British accent.

You did?

Yes I'm doing work trade here. I'm from Germany. Where are you from?

America, I said.

That's so cool, she said. I want to go there someday. Do you want to hang out after dinner? It's so boring here.

Yes yes yes.

It was almost summer, which meant the sun didn't set until seven-thirty pm. Nina took me to a field half a mile from the hostel. She smiled a lot, her green eyes sweet and intense in a way that let me be exactly where I was, forgetting all the moments that pushed behind me, my ghost temporarily muted.

It's a private farm, but if you lay low in the grass no one can see you, she said. I come here a lot to smoke.

We lay side-by-side and she lit up a joint. The grass was tall and itchy but smelled like flowers and blustered in melodic gusts with the wind, reminding us to shhhh. I took a big hit off the joint. I held the smoke in my lungs until I coughed, which made her laugh which made me laugh. We blew smoke at the sky, watching it escape and dissolve into nothing as our heads became light and free. I wanted to hold her hand, but it felt too soon. When someone looks like someone you loved, the threads get crossed and tangled, knotting up so delicately you don't realize it.

Do you have a boyfriend? she asked.

No. Do you?

Yes, but I hate him.

Why do you hate him?

He's annoying and very stupid, she said, blowing more smoke out as she talked.

I laughed. Why don't you break up with him?

I don't know. It seems like too much work, she laughed with me.

Have you ever dated girls? I asked.

No. But I'm not against it.

You should. You seem gay.

This made her laugh more. She passed me the joint.

How old are you? she asked.

Twenty-three. How old are you?

Sixteen.

Oh, I thought you were at least twenty.

No, I'm on a high school exchange program.

We were stoned and laughing in hiccups and loops. I decided against trying to hold her hand and, in my mind, instead of calling her hot Nina I started calling her cool teenage friend Nina. As I shifted my stance, I felt space and a small wave of relief grow around me. Crushes take a lot of work. When the potential for romance dissipates, friendship gets to be uninhibited and deeper.

I'm starving, she said. Let's go to the kitchen. I have a key so we can eat anything we want.

We walked back to the hostel in the dark, looking up at the stars and down the dim lit cobblestone streets. The moon was new so the stars shone as bright as they could shine, tiny bursts like Christmas lights in wild patterns. The air smelled like the perfect beginnings of summer, slight lavender blooms and the leftover heat of the day baked into the earth. I took a deep breath and held it in for as long as I could. I wanted to swallow those moments and wrap my organs in summer air and friend love.

The hostel was dark and quiet. Nina pulled out her keys and led us into the kitchen. We giggled like the teenager she was, opening the cupboards and pulling out jars of pickles and olives and bread and cheese and jam. We opened all the jars at once, spreading hunks of bread out all over the stainless-steel counter, making crumbs and sticky jam blobs and rolling olive pits and cheese smudges around our fingers as we stuffed our stoned mouths. We ate and laughed more and even though she was only sixteen, I fell in love with her for the next hour and forgot about everything else in the world. There are so many gradients of love.

I made you a snack for the train, Nina said the next morning.

She walked me to the train station and handed me a container full of cold spaghetti. I tried not to cry about her thoughtfulness and her Margaret face and the way I was platonically so in love with her. I could've stayed longer but my guts were persuading me to keep momentum toward Ireland. Even when there's a goal, the goal is never the end. I knew Ireland was not a stopping place. But it was a resting place to catch my breath and find space. I hugged her and took a picture of her in front of a giant wall clock and said goodbye. She watched as the train pulled away, waving furiously like a little kid. I waved furiously back.

I ate the spaghetti with my fingers on the way to Liverpool, knowing my lips and cheeks were turning orange from the sauce and not giving a shit. It was salty and tangy and perfect. I wiped my mouth on my sleeve, put my spongy headphones over my ears, and pressed play.

And if you wonder what I would do / I would do anything if I could / you know I would / I would for you.

I looked for her on the train. I took a deep breath in and smelled for the cigarette, the vagina slime. My nose searched. I wanted the smoke, her smoke. I wanted her to see I was okay. I had Nina. I had Konrad. I had Ireland. I wanted her and I thought of her when I heard the song, any of the songs. There are people we need to let go of, sometimes because they no longer want us. It's best to forget. But all we want to do is remember, for them to see us forgetting them, remembering. She wasn't on that train. I closed my eyes and thought of her face, singing. Perry Farrell's voice became her voice.

I would for you.

That day we all gathered behind the swings at the far end of the park, smoking a joint and watching kids swing their bodies through the air, laughing and talking about being small, how free we felt no longer being kids. Even though we were kids. We were such kids, so small in our beings. Someone pressed play on a portable boom box and Jane's Addiction blasted across the playground, the soundtrack of our teen-hood. The tape got flipped from side A to side B to side A over and over until we decided it was good, passing the tape insert around admiring pictures of the band and reading along with printed lyrics, folding, unfolding, turning it over and smoothing it out. I lay with my head in her lap looking up at the clouds, occasionally glancing at her perfect chin and the shape of her nostrils. We passed a cigarette back and forth and I wanted the world to get stuck in that moment forever.

8.

The guidebook said to take a taxi from the train station to the ferry that would go all the way to Dublin. The taxi driver dropped me off at a deserted, industrial dock.

You sure you want to be dropped off here? he said.

I think so, I said. The guidebook hadn't steered me wrong yet.

A warm breeze moved the water in soft waves against the shore, rocking boats as if to put them to sleep. I looked up at the sky. Fluffy white clouds and the sun coming and going, seagulls riding waves of air and cawing into the wind assured me I would be okay. When the outside is peaceful, the inside can relax. I saw the sign for the ferry and my gut told me this was the right place, another new beginning, an essential adventure that would propel me into the next.

I got on the boat, which was also deserted, and enormous. Its interior was full of blue velvet plush couches that pressed up against giant, slanted windows overlooking a deck. There was a cafeteria with metal tables and chairs and a thin set of spiral stairs leading up to a series of closed rooms, for those who wanted to sleep. This Love Boat was the opposite of the boat from Ostend to Dover, a bumpy two-hour ride on hard, plastic seats squished together, enclosed in a tight capsule, which was my only experience of boats in Europe so far. I found a seat near some bay windows and settled in. I waited. One by one, passengers began to board the boat, all of them, men. My mind was worried, but my guts, again, told me I was in the right place. Mental fear squashed to make room for a deeper version of myself. The line between guts and brains is elusive, sometimes making it difficult to decipher which is which, one overriding the other. In that moment though, my guts were on the bullhorn. Soon the boat was full of men plus me, and we were off.

I leaned my big pack against the dark blue velvet seat and stretched my legs out toward it, resting my feet on its frame. The sun shone bright and the water looked sparkly out the bay windows. I thought about her, the blue couch, the blue water, the blue sky and her blue eyes.

I closed my eyes and heard her voice, sad and angry with me, but really at her mother, who took refuge as a Buddhist after we finished high school and left home. I thought it was cool of her mom. She was trying to turn her life around.

It's not fucking cool, she said. She goes to retreats all the time instead of visiting me. All she cares about is herself.

The fight happened after she overheard a conversation I had with my own mom. We lived in a one-bedroom apartment and shared a phone line. Besides the bathroom, the bedroom door was the only door we had to close for privacy, which we never closed because we shared the closet. We were tangled from the outside in a way we didn't mean to be and tangled from the inside in a way we couldn't control. I loved her and hated her and wanted to be her and wanted her to want to be me. She ignored me for two days after the phone call, talking at me only in snaps, sharp and icy, shooting daggers from her hard eyes.

What the hell? I finally said.

I knew it wasn't about me. But that knowing didn't make it hurt any less.

The pattern was for me to coax and push and poke and get soft, look into her eyes with love, apologize for being okay. That time was no different than any other. She admitted her jealousy of my relationship with my mom, hearing my mom's voice messages on the answering machine, light and sweet and the easy way we talked on the phone. But what she knew of our relationship was incomplete. She never came to my house when we were in high school. She didn't see how I fought with my mom. She didn't see my challenges and she never asked and I never told her. That was a place we intersected. Neither of us shared without being asked, and neither of us asked much. Maybe we didn't want to be intrusive, or maybe we were just too self-absorbed. Or both.

The only people who know the insides of a relationship are the people in it. All relationships, especially with family, are complex and layered. But I said the wrong thing.

My mom's hard too, I said.

You have no idea. You're so spoiled. She rolled her eyes and huffed.

Tears welled in my throat. You're mean and uninformed, I said.

Oh please, she said.

It wasn't about the words. Words matter and they don't. The feelings behind her words were so much bigger than the sounds coming out of her mouth. The way her eyelids sharpened around her eyes, the anger she projected, the anger in her face, the blades from her pale eyes, was what hurt. We fought. The same fight over and over. She smashed a plate down on the kitchen linoleum and stormed around the apartment, stomping her feet, huffing, then slammed the bedroom door and blasted PJ Harvey at full volume, so that even my apologies were drowned out.

Time was the only way through.

For the rest of the six months we lived there, we found ceramic shards everywhere. One night I was walking barefoot in the middle of the night to go to the bathroom, half asleep, and felt a sharp pinch in the sole of my foot, which I was too tired to care about. In the morning, we found bloody footprints from the toilet to the bed. She wiped up the blood, then used her tweezers to carefully remove the shards and made an herbal compress to heal the wound. She didn't often apologize with words. When she did, her words felt thin and forced. Words were not our language. But I felt her remorse through her herbs soothing my skin.

All the things, all the ways of being, all at once.

Both and.

9.

What are you going to do in Ireland? A round, red-faced man woke me from my trance. He looked kind, his energy genuinely interested. I opened my eyes and looked at him too long with a blank face. The sun was coming in hot and strong through the picture window behind me. I reached for the small pocket at the top of my backpack and pulled out a package of dark chocolate. It was completely melted.

The name's Roger, he extended a hand.

I shook his hand and sat up.

I'm going to check out Dublin and from there I was hoping to find a farm to work on, I said.

You don't say. My neighbor in the village I'm from near Kildare, has a farm. I'll call him up right now.

Roger pulled out a thick, industrial looking cell phone and attached a wiry antenna. Hello Frank, I've got a worker for you, he said.

He handed me the phone and said, He wants to talk to you.

Frank's voice was gravelly and faint, like he was far away and too busy to talk. He only asked my name, then said I could come work on the farm whenever I was ready, to have Roger let him know when I'd be arriving. It was a quick conversation before he said goodbye. I handed the phone back to Roger and thanked him.

That was easy, I said.

Well, you know, nothing should be too much of a struggle in life if you're a good person. I always say, if it's too hard, you're going in the wrong direction.

I smiled. Do you know how long this boat ride is?

Bout eight hours, he said.

We were an hour in. I felt the shock on my face.

He nodded and said, Yes indeed it's quite long. Surprising to see you chose this one.

It does seem strange that I'm the only female on the boat.

Most tourists take the overnight, he said. This boat is for the trolley drivers. But don't worry, the restaurant will be open soon. Do you have any food tokens?

I shook my head no, thinking about my melted chocolate.

Here, I have a bunch. We get them each time we make a trip to a new job. Roger handed me a stack of coins.

Are you sure?

Just take 'em. You'll have to eat, won't you?

By then, a few of the other truck drivers had started to gather around. Some of them offered more food tokens and one guy said I could go up and sleep in his room. He was one of the younger guys and, though he seemed as kind as the rest of them, my gut said no. My mind also said no. I thanked everyone and watched the sky turn bright pink and orange as the sun began to sink.

When the boat finally pulled into the dock, Roger said he could drive me to a hostel in Dublin then pick me up two days later to take me to Frank's farm. I had no other plans. Even if you don't make plans, things happen, open space filling itself to stay connected. The trolley garage was just around the corner from the dock and all the boat passengers herded toward it. Roger helped me up into the driver's seat, which was really the passenger seat, and drove us down narrow, tree-lined roads into the city. I looked out the window up into the sky, twinkling stars and a moon starting to present itself. I was happy to let the space fill in on its own, without effort but with full trust. I thought about what Roger said about trying too hard.

Less effort creates more ease.

The hostel was down a windy side street full of coffee houses, pubs, and small shops. There were Andy Warhol style murals of Sinead O'Connor, Bono, and other famous Irish rock stars painted on the walls, and a group of people who looked to be around my age sitting around a mosaic-tiled table in the lobby drinking beers. No one seemed to be traveling with a hair dryer. The girl at the counter didn't even have hair to dry. Her head was shaved and she had a thin hoop piercing her nostril. She smiled and showed me to a room full of bunk beds, pointing out the communal bathroom down the hall. I put my bag down on a bed to claim it, then went out to the bar in the lobby where I noticed a skinny, shaggy haired boy reading tarot cards.

Mind if I watch? I asked.

He smiled. I'll do yours next if you want, he said.

I nodded and watched as he flipped cards and breathed deep and calm, as though he was breathing the images into his body and projecting them onto the screen behind his eyes. He wasn't thinking. He was feeling, channeling. He tucked a tuft of hair behind his ear and I noticed a small, rainbow triangle earring. You only notice those things if you need to, how subtle symbols of commonality convey safety and ease. I felt my shoulder blades move down my back. My neck released. I didn't even realize it was tight.

When my turn came, he told me to shuffle the cards and focus. He said, Think about something you want to know, a question maybe.

I looked at the cards, felt their smooth edges around my fingers. The deck was called, The Herbal Tarot. Each card had the plant of a medicinal herb in addition to its tarot symbols. Plants made me think of her: herbs and DIY medicines. I closed my eyes and shuffled, thinking about the mugwort, calendula, comfrey, and valerian hanging on strings around that tiny kitchen we shared. The nettles and raspberry leaves she boiled to make tea for our menstrual cramps. The dusty crumbs of dried plants all over the counters and in between the pages of her herb books. Pouring infused alcohol tinctures into tiny bottles, blasting Babes in Toyland and dancing around the kitchen. The apartment smelled of earth and rain, fragrant and grounded the way she wanted to be. The way she sometimes was.

I couldn't think of a question. I just thought of her, of the good times laced with bitter edges. When people die, the memories change. Some parts get brighter, some fade. Some memories get lost, and some are not true. Memories don't live in our minds as much as in our bodies and hearts. I feel it first, then attach the story. I wondered how much our stories would line up. I wanted to tell her stories of us that I remembered and ask if she remembered them the same way. But we never had time to reminisce. That's the worst part. There's no one to confirm any of it happened, and no one to argue with the way things were. I had to trust myself or make things up to fill in the gaps.

I gave him back the cards and he said, Cut the deck with your less dominant hand into three piles, then put them all back together into one pile. Don't think, just feel where the cards want to split.

I put my left hand on the deck and pressed my fingers into its sides, the thin edges denting my skin, ridges like a million moments all stacked and pressed together, each its own defined thing but helpless without the whole. Relativity is so hard to come by when it's isolated, but there is no whole without each single one, each individual piece.

He pulled three cards off the top and lined them up in a row in front of me: XII the suspended person with kelp, VI the lovers with parsley, and the three of swords with pleurisy root. It seemed too obvious. But things should be obvious. That's what not trying hard means. Letting go.

Ease inside of effort.

Softening inside of struggle.

Someone has recently passed. A girl, he said.

I looked up at him. He was still looking down at the cards. My heart started beating hard, pushing against my sternum, and my hands felt hot. In my body, inside the pockets of air moving around my skin, I knew she was there. His eyebrows creased and he looked up, not at my face but past me, behind me.

She's with you sometimes, he said.

He didn't ask questions or wait for me to confirm anything.

I see straight black hair, maybe glasses and a nose ring, he continued.

I turned to look where he was looking behind me. I saw her. Or maybe I didn't. Ghosts are like memories, they're ethereal and their reality depends on emotional sensation. I looked down at the cards, then turned back again to see if she was there. She was. She wasn't. I didn't feel sad. Sad is too simple. But I cried, my tears falling heavy onto the cards.

Sorry, I said, wiping the water off with my hand.

He smiled a kind smile, the way you do when you're trying to be supportive and positive. I told him the story of us. He nodded his head and listened unsurprised, like he knew everything I was going to say before I said it. He knew I loved her the moment I saw her, but that the love was complicated, and maybe not love at all.

10.

We met in AP English class sophomore year and bonded over loving the nerdy teacher, who was rumored to have had a mental breakdown in front of the class five years before we were there. Everyone made fun of the teacher behind her back, but we thought her quirky was endearing. We never skipped English to smoke in the bathroom like we did during math and science. We knew writing was cool before it was cool, reading lyrics from unfolded tape case inserts to each other over bathroom stall cigarettes, never getting caught. That nerdy teacher, her glasses crooked on her scrunched face, her shirt always halfway tucked and wrinkled, cared only about our poetry, even when we came in late smelling of smoke. The only thing we cared about too, along with music and each other.

She was born old, ahead of the years of her life. I wanted to live with her in the strangeness and the knowing of what was next, what was cool before it was cool.

Meet me in the alley, she said one Saturday afternoon.

The piercing gun was shiny and small. She pulled a faux diamond stud out of her pocket and popped it into the gun, clicking it a few times in the air.

Pierce my nose, I said.

She smiled and slid one side of the gun into my nostril.

Ready? she said.

Yeah do it. When I breathe out, I said.

I took a deep breath in, held it for a few seconds, and exhaled. The gun clicked and I heard a little crack, the stud breaking the skin of my nose. Impaled cartilage. My eyes watered. It hurt but I didn't care. I touched the jewelry and she smiled and said it looked perfect.

11.

Tarot boy listened without words, then explained the cards. He said:

The suspended person is about seeing things from a different perspective, being open to another angle. Turn things upside down and the whole world changes. What are you hung up on, literally, and how can you suspend your disbelief of what is happening, knowing there is something else you don't know? Loss jars us into a reality we couldn't imagine seeing. Kelp is salty like tears, emotional, growing in the water, under the surface, subconscious or otherworldly. This card is about connecting beyond what you can see and what you believe to be true.

The lovers represent the duality of head and heart, thinking and feeling, the union of opposites. Relationship with other is obvious, but there is also the mirror of the self, which is reflected within the relationship, and the responsibility of action in our choices. Cooperation. No one can make you feel any certain way. There is no conflict or love between two if only one side participates. Parsley is digestive. It moves things through the body and eliminates bitterness and excess water. Tears and hardship. When we relate, or more so when we connect and communicate truth, things become clear and stagnation dissolves.

I listened and nodded and breathed. He looked up at me occasionally, his eyes in my eyes. A conversation isn't always both people talking.

He continued:

You can see the three of swords is a pierced, tender heart. This is the card of sorrow, heartbreak, and hurt feelings. Swords are heady and sharp and as they puncture the heart, it's as though the heart—as the emotional body—gets imprisoned by the wild mind. The mind takes over, forcing itself down into the body without regard for the heart's own depth of experience. Pleurisy root heals inflammation in the chest. It helps the body breathe and expand. This card is about acknowledging heartache, feeling what needs to be felt, not what you think you should feel, so that the heartache can move out of the body. Breathe out the ache.

No loss is clean and easy, he said. Forgotten memories tend to reappear with new emotion. You don't have to hold any of it in any certain way. This moment in your life is about letting things be without trying to make them something else. Remember the love and also the pain.

I looked at the cards, his words hanging in the air around each one. I probably could've gotten any of the cards in the deck in any combination and still felt all the feelings. Art helps. So does believing in magic. I thanked him for the reading and he offered me a hug, which I accepted. The heat of his torso against mine felt like a weighted blanket. I felt his unattached love in that moment, and I extended mine back.

That night, I put learn tarot on my list of things to do when I got home. I thought of the three of swords card, that lush red heart stabbed symmetrically three times, impending gray clouds closing in around it, while I lay in my thin bunk bed looking up at the mural of The Cranberries painted on the ceiling. Dolores O'Riordan's eyes, my eyes, connected. Her face started to move like she was breathing. I thought of her lyrics, watched them come out of her painted mouth:

There's no need to argue anymore / I gave all I could but it left me so sore / And the thing that makes me sad / is the one thing that I had / I knew, I knew, I'd lose you.

In the morning, I opened my eyes to the sun blazing in through a small, high window. Dolores was still looking at me, now still and quiet. I packed my sleeping bag and headed to the café for coffee and a biscuit. Roger was set to pick me up soon.

12.

Hop up, Roger said.

He threw my bag into the back of the truck and I got into the seat next to his. We drove through the rolling green hills of the Irish countryside, passing farms and stopping in the middle of tiny highway roads for occasional sheep crossings. Roger was a kind, small town guy. In America, I wouldn't hitch a ride with a random truck driver I met on a boat. I probably wouldn't be on a boat in the first place. But in Ireland, the landscape of people and society moved in the space between. Culture and circumstance weave in subtle ways through our blood. Maybe we're safer when we don't know what the danger is. Or when we don't need to know. I was untethered and free with nothing but a dirty backpack and a potential ghost to call mine. Ireland was a sigh I had been waiting to release.

When we arrived at Farmer Frank's farm, Roger wished me luck in my adventures and I thanked him for making my journey smoother. He smiled, his pink cheeks turning hot red. We shook hands, held hands really, a shake without the shake, for a moment too long without being awkward. Then he drove away, down the windy, dirt path back toward the main road. I watched the dusty cloud from his truck rise and chase behind him like tumbleweed. I waved long after he was gone.

Don't forget this moment.

Remember this moment.

Farmer Frank greeted me with a nod, a hello, and a, follow me, which I did. He led me into an old stone house, the kind I imagined everyone in Ireland lived in. There was an ancient wood-burning stove in the center of the living room with a sofa and two ragged, plaid recliner chairs facing the stove, and no electricity. There were four small bedrooms crammed together, sharing walls; one for middle-aged Farmer Frank, one for his aging mother, one for me, and one for the other farm worker, Cullen. Frank didn't shake my hand and he didn't ask me questions. I could feel his guard, so I didn't ask questions either. Feelings are so much stronger than words. And also, words are so resilient and durable. The juxtapose follows me everywhere.

You can get settled in and rest. We get up at six a.m. to head to the field down the road and get working. We'll have a little breakfast first, some toast and jam with eggs. That all right for you? he said.

Sounds good, I said.

I nodded too big, like I was trying to prove my words with my body. I realized this farm was the real deal, a real farm. I was going to have to earn my food and lodging with hard work. I wasn't prepared to get up at dawn. I was nervous. But also, I was excited for newness. The night passed quickly and before the sun came up, I woke to the sound of a ringing bell, the kind that signifies it's time for a meal. The room was dark and smelled of wood smoke burning in the stove, filling the tiny house. The smell was comforting, but the air was still cold enough to see my breath. I wrapped myself in a hoodie and slipped on two pairs of socks. We sat around a rickety wooden table crunching toast in silence. I loved it. I felt alive and real, like I was doing something important. I made sure to swipe my table crumbs onto my plate with the side of my hand, to keep my space clean. I wanted them to know that I was respectful.

The farm was a ten-minute drive from the house, just on the edge of the village. There we met Emma, a young blond girl who lived in an old trailer on the land and worked on the farm for the summer. Farmer Frank paired me up with her to show me the ropes. Emma had familiar eyes, blue glass, shiny and warm.

Her eyes in Emma's eyes.

Her eyes everywhere.

Emma caught me looking too long. She smiled and said, I know the feeling.

What? I said. Oh sorry.

You're not looking at me. There's someone else. Close but far?

I nodded.

She shrugged.

Come on, let's get to work, she said.

We walked up and down rows of carrots and beets, carefully pulling out tiny weeds next to the tiny sprouts. This was how we spent the morning. By noon the sun was hot overhead and I regretted my two pairs of socks. We took a break for lunch at an outdoor picnic table. Emma's eyes caught my eyes throughout the lunchtime conversation, always smiling, but she never asked again. She let me look, let me drift into memories through my own sensory experience. A color, a smell, a sound, a person can take you all the way back, leaving the boundary of skin and body. But it wasn't really my mind that drifted. It was her. She pulled me whenever she knew I was vulnerable enough to be taken.

We all became chattier over lunch, as though the sun broke down everyone's walls. Everyone except for Farmer Frank. I didn't expect him to suddenly open up, and I didn't judge him for his tight boundaries. Boundaries create edges, a home, places to press up against and feel real. I already knew he had secrets, even though I didn't know anything about them.

Cullen talked about how he had lived with Farmer Frank for the past three years, helping out on the farm during the week and living back in the city on the weekends. He was a handsome younger man, tall and muscular, a few years older than me. I had a feeling we would be close friends if we lived in the same town. There was something familiar about him, like I couldn't say anything that would offend him. Emma said she was there on summer break from school in Dublin, working to save money for the school year. She was studying agriculture. She was only an inch taller than me, but her hands were surprisingly big and rough, displaying her work and love of touching the earth. She had the kind of hands that get washed and scrubbed often, but never look fully clean, stained with work, dirt tattooed into the creases. I told them where I'd been, and what I'd seen, the boats, the people, the beer, the sheep crossing roads. No one asked where I was planning to go next and I was relieved. There is a subtle balance between not asking enough and asking too much.

That night I slept hard. Work hard, eat hard, sleep hard. I slept like that for the entire week, each night a deep and almost dreamless rest. We woke early each morning, ate, worked, ate, worked, went back to the house, ate, and went to bed with occasional showers in between. No one complained. No one talked about living a different life. Being a farmer was harder than any job I'd ever had. And also, it was beautiful and distracting and breathtaking and rewarding. My mind stayed focused on the smell of clean air and tiny plants, subtle summer smokiness coming from distant wood burning stoves and trees releasing their delicate perfumes. I worked quietly in the meditation of consistency, and by the light of an oil lamp each evening, I wrote about the day in my journal before going to sleep. It was magical, and after a week I was ready for something else.

I saw her outside my open window as I lay in bed on the last night I spent at Farmer Frank's. She was looking at me from a distance through the window, her hair blowing in the kind of wind that comes just before rain.

The smell of wet earth.

The feeling of storm on my skin.

I knew it was coming. A breeze picked up and blew the thin curtain up and all around. I yelled out to her to go inside, that the rain was coming and it was going to be big. I knew she could hear me, her eyes in my eyes far and also immediate, but she didn't move. I heard my voice scream her name. I heard her name, then Emma's name, my mouth closed as I called out from the inside on the inside. Like a horror movie girl standing stoic in the dark, changing form each time the thunder crashes. But it wasn't a horror and it wasn't a movie. Just a storm I dreamed up or lived through without being alone. Never alone, always missing someone. Both. Neither.

I breathed in the rain air.

I breathed it in and let it out over and over.

We're going to the coast of Galway this weekend, Farmer Frank said. Would you like to come?

It was a perfect invitation.

Yes, I said. Yes please yes.

Farmer Frank, Cullen, and I rode the two hours to Galway city in Frank's old Datsun. Emma stayed back to keep an eye on things. I wasn't sad at the thought of never seeing her again. She was too close, too much of a reminder. I couldn't see her as her individual self. Somewhere in history we're all related, that web that makes some people look like, or feel like, other people without knowing. Doppelganger eyes. The tangle of memory was constantly tugging at my sleeves. Time loops, parallel and just out of reach. Moving and shifting gave me space to dive into people and places without consequence. Maybe there's less accountability this way. But also, there's more space to not get stuck.

Both and.

Both. And.

When we arrived, Farmer Frank said we had a couple of hours before meeting up with Mark, a friend who would be taking us on a hike up a mountain and then to his house on a nearby island.

I have some business to do. Go explore the town and we'll meet back up here at one, he said.

I'll show you the town, Cullen said to me.

We walked around the cobblestone streets and I took pictures of every cozy, brightly colored storefront. We danced to street musicians playing Irish jigs. We looked through shop windows at trinkets and tourist shirts. And finally, we stopped into a pub for snacks and creamy Guinness, a meal in a can. Cullen noticed a bracelet I was wearing made out of an old bike tube with a metal loop attached, like a cuff.

Where'd you find that gem? he asked.

My friend makes things out of recycled bicycle tire tubes. Here try it on, I said.

He wrapped the bracelet around his thin wrist.

It's just so cool, he said.

Keep it, I said.

Really?

Yeah, it looks good on you.

Cullen held up his wrist, turning it side to side to catch the light in the metal loop. We clinked our beers and gulped them down.

When we met back up with Farmer Frank, Cullen glowed about the bracelet to Frank. I noticed a flicker between them, like a flirtation, a sweet, shared secret. Farmer Frank was slow to smile, but in that moment, I saw a hint of movement around the sides of his mouth, his cheeks lifting so slightly. His eyes glittering into Cullen's eyes.

Glitter sparkle energy.

Frank drove us to the edge of town at the base of the hills where we met up with Mark, the hiking guide. He led us, along with two other men, up to a peak with a dramatic three-sixty view. The land was open rolling hills and smooth, like it was carved and sanded intentionally to make us feel majestic. As we hiked, the air stretched my lungs until they burned. It felt good, the feeling of reaching the edge, then pushing past it. Everyone breathed deep. When we got to the top, no one moved or spoke for a long time. I closed my eyes and she arrived.

I hadn't thought of her yet that day, distracted by newness. But at that moment, I felt the weight of her fire. I remembered to remember. She pressed down on my chest, like she was mad that I hadn't been paying her enough attention. Her eyes burned behind mine. The singing crows overhead grew loud. I looked up. A crow swooped around my head, close enough for me to see its eyes, sharp blue. I tried to follow her, but she was too close, then gone, too far. The wind picked up and I closed my eyes again, breathed out in heavy sighs.

Blue eyed crow.

Crows have better eyesight than humans, four primary colors to our three. Some people think crows possess metacognition, remember people, and are more intelligent than primates. Maybe this is why they live so fearlessly among people. She liked everything black.

Human crow.

Shape shifter.

The places we intersect, weave together in thin strands with tight curls to latch like the tendrils of cucumber plants, so delicate and also, so strong. Velcro.

13.

We had lawn seats at the first Lollapalooza, sitting up on a grassy hill. Once we found our spot, our friend passed out acid tabs, tiny squares of paper infused with a drop of liquid LSD.

Leave it on your tongue for half an hour and then swallow it, he said.

He smiled and stuck out his tongue to show us his tab.

We weren't scared. We were never scared, even when we were. We knew not to be, to convince each other to stay alive and lean into fear, holding hands, staying connected. We pressed the tabs into the flesh of our tongues and laughed.

After an hour, the grass began to breathe, rolling up and down, smooth and happy, the sound of wind like clapping chimes and Buddhist bowls. My body tingled. I said her name. She looked at me and said my name. We started laughing. Her eyes crying dollops of tears synced with mine, like I was looking in a mirror.

The water of her eyes made of salty ocean.

Look at the clouds, I said.

The sky is alive, she said.

Look at my hand, I said. All the lines are moving.

It's like palmistry, she said, where the lines tell you what your life will be. Maybe my life isn't determined. Maybe there is no fate. Maybe nothing is planned.

We put our palms together, mine small, her fingers long, overlapping. She could hold the world. The crowd started cheering, screaming, clapping, whistling, stage lights going dark, then flashing colors. Giant puppets of naked ladies on fire rose up on the stage.

Drums boomed. Then guitars, and Perry Farrell's voice:

I am skin and bones, I am pointy nose / But it motherfuckin' makes me try / Makes me try, and that ain't wrong / I'll tell you why…There ain't no right! / Ain't no wrong now, ain't no right…

She leaned into me and put her lips on mine. We kissed for the length of the song into the next song and the next one. I wanted the moment to stretch in an endless loop. My body felt light, the wind moving through my flesh, warm and perfect. Tears rolled down the skin of my face, but I wasn't sad, just all the emotion trapped in my muscles was being released. When the kiss was over, I opened my eyes, the feeling of a weightless, seamless, dream with no past and the future exactly where it's supposed to be. Floating in her salt water.

Her eyes my eyes all one thing.

Everything different.

A new beginning.

14.

As we walked down the hill, one of the guys expressed his excitement for white wine spritzers back at the house after the long hike. Everyone laughed and agreed. I looked at Cullen and he winked at me. I nodded. White wine spritzers.

Mark's house was a thirty-minute drive from the hills, across a bridge into a cluster of islands. As we drove, the road signs went from English, to English and Irish, to Irish only.

We don't call it Gaelic in Ireland, Frank said. That's the English word. In Ireland it's called Irish.

I leaned toward the driver's seat to listen. Frank didn't say much, but when he did, it was important.

The language, he said, is getting lost. But the farther from cities you go, the more it's used. The islands are trying to stay true to our culture. When language gets lost, culture gets diluted. That's why the further out we get, the less English signs you see. It's meant to keep appropriation out. But some of the kids these days don't even understand Irish. It's heartbreaking. There is conflict in the schools of whether or not to keep teaching it.

The islands are not meant for tourists, Cullen said. They're our best secret. Only Irish people who've been around for generations live out here. You're lucky to get to see this place.

Mark told me to close my eyes on the drive so that I wouldn't remember the way, I said.

Mark was smiling when he said it, but I felt truth behind his words. Frank and Cullen laughed. And they nodded in agreement. I didn't close my eyes, but I don't have a good sense of direction anyway. Instead, I leaned back and looked out the window, watching the landscape become more pristine with each mile. Less houses, more space, ocean water and seagulls coasting on wind drifts. I thought about the Irish signs, words with letters that don't sound the way they sound in my head, how language is meant to connect people and also, to protect them.

Mark's house was small and low, a single-story cottage made of mossy stone and wood. The neighbor's house was barely visible from his property. I felt like I was in a fairytale, understanding why Mark didn't want me to remember the way there. The outside was a magical, dreamy Tolkien story, soft boulder cliffs, strong against the rushing sea and vivid green hills in all other directions. The landscape looked like the kind of painting hung in a hotel lobby. Inside the house was different; white wine spritzers and walls covered in photographs of Mark dressed in full drag with six-inch stiletto heeled boots, giant teased hair, and a deep shade of red lipstick.

I knew these men didn't know I was safe to hold their homosexuality, tangled in my own. I knew Farmer Frank came up in a time in which he had to hide who he was. And I knew his feeling of safety with others happened only when he decided others were safe. I took my spritzer over to Cullen and asked him to take a walk with me toward the water. We found a spot to sit near the edge of a low stone wall where the water lapped rhythmically against the shore. I told him the bracelet was meant to be like a leather cuff used in bondage play, which he already knew. Then I asked him about his relationship with Frank.

It's complicated, he said. We're all gay you know.

I raised my glass and cheers'd his.

I know, I said. I am too.

He smiled, not surprised. I didn't tell him about her.

I love him and he loves me, he said. But for him, it's internalized more. He came up in a time when he wasn't allowed to be out. Even now, at his age, they all feel cautious. Taking care of his mum is a good excuse for him not to be married. And I'm glad I can help. But sometimes, I do wish we could just be who we are out in the world.

Do you think you'll ever move away? I said.

You know, the future is open and the present is quite okay right now. We manage. I manage alright.

I nodded.

I'm not unhappy, he said. You have to lean into the good bits. Love what you have and more love will grow from that.

Indeed.

We watched the sun set over the water and drank until our glasses were empty.

15.

The next morning, Cullen drove me to the Galway bus station. We hugged like old friends and as I closed the car door and waved, he held up his wrist and moved it side to side, jiggling the metal loop on the bike tube cuff. I smiled and thought about the spark I'd seen between him and Frank when he showed Frank the bracelet, the way their gaze sealed bright in the knowing that happens between two people. You never know what really goes on inside a relationship, and that not knowing is what creates the bond.

Inside joke.

Exclusive bubble.

I got on a bus to County Cork to meet the next farmers. I found them in Farmer Frank's WOOFF directory and called to set up a meeting before we left for Galway. Claudia met me at the station in Bandon. She had told me on the phone that she was pregnant, so I recognized her immediately. She was Italian, she had said, and her partner, Joseph, was English. They had a six-year-old boy named Liam and their farm was a make-shift tree farm. I didn't know what that meant, but it sounded completely different from Farmer Frank's, which was my only requirement. Keep changing.

Claudia pulled up in a small, rust colored Toyota Corolla. She hobbled out and offered to take my bag. I immediately declined. She was so pregnant I wondered how she fit into the tiny car. I offered her a square of melted chocolate, which had re-hardened in the cool morning Irish air. She accepted. We got into the Corolla and she drove us out of town through windy roads, passing farmscapes covered in clusters of fluffy sheep. I rolled down my window and breathed in the clean air. The best air I ever smelled. I thought I might never leave Ireland.

Our place is unusual, she said.

I like unusual.

Oh good, she laughed. It's sort of a commune. There are no actual Irish people living there. Just people from around Europe and a woman from New Zealand.

How did that happen?

It's an expat thing. You'll see, she said.

She smiled wide. Her skin was perfectly tan and she had a soft Italian accent that sounded like an Enya song, gentle and easy. I wanted to be around her voice for a long time, to sink into it like a beanbag chair, soothing and held. We turned onto a gravel road and she put the car into second gear to slow down. The crunchy sound of car wheels on gravel, like feet on leaves. We parked in front of a small cabin where Joseph and Liam were sitting on wooden porch steps, waving. Claudia opened her door and Liam immediately jumped up to meet her. She introduced us, then introduced me to Joseph, who said he'd show me around. He offered to take my bag. I accepted this time. Joseph walked me down a short, wooded path to a yurt.

This is yours while you're here, he said.

He opened a slanted door and put my pack inside. The place was dark but cozy, with a small bed, a wood stove, and a desk. The roof was shaped like a cone, all the slats exposed and pointing up to a round skylight. Christmas twinkle lights were woven through the slats. It was janky and beautiful. I was excited to have a private place of my own for the first time in a long time.

Come on I'll show you the rest of the land, he said.

There was a small outhouse a few steps from the yurt with a moon sliver carved into the door and yellow stars painted around it. From there, down the hill, was the rest of the community. A few more cabins, an Airstream trailer, an old converted school bus, and a garden in the center of it all. Behind all the structures was a huge field of wildflowers, then a dense patch of woods.

There are trails through those woods, nice to walk through when you feel like it, Joseph said. You'll meet everyone else soon. Come on, I'll show you the tree farm.

On the other side of the cabin where he lived with Claudia and Liam, opposite from the rest of the land, was another short dirt path. At its end sat a small patch of land, bigger than a personal garden, but not what I think of as farm size, especially compared to Farmer Frank's place. He said he was growing tree saplings to sell. It was their business. He saw the confused look on my face.

It's a trial run. We have to make money in order to stay on the land. They'll be ready for Christmas we hope, he said.

Joseph was older than me, but young. He was tall and thin and had a tender smile and sparkly eyes. I told him about Farmer Frank's farm. He assured me my time at this place would be quite different.

That night, I lay in the small bed under a patchwork quilt looking up at the skylight, tiny glowing stars, glimmering. I thought about the time we went to the planetarium, where the entire domed ceiling is the sky, projected constellations moving slowly so you feel like you're floating in space. The main attraction was the laser light show set to Pink Floyd's Dark Side of the Moon album. We got stoned in the car before we went in and squeezed eye drops into our red eyes so no one would know. When the lasers started, I got nauseous. We laughed because we were stoned, but also, she put her hand on my shoulder and said, Close your eyes and take a deep breath. Now open your mouth.

She pulled a peppermint spirits tincture out of her bag and dropped a few drops onto my tongue. The shock of coolness immediately soothed my nausea and made my mouth water. I have always loved mint. I opened my eyes and smiled. She was smiling back, the color in her watery Aquarius eyes squishing around, waves in the ocean, shooting stars moving around the speckles of her eye constellations.

I couldn't sleep. I was calm but my mind wouldn't shift. I read somewhere that you should get out of bed and do something when you have insomnia, to relieve the stress of not being able to sleep, and that putting your bare feet on the ground helps to reset your mind. I got out of bed and opened the slanted yurt door. It creaked in a satisfying, old wooden door kind of way. The moon was a tiny crescent fingernail, like the one painted on the outhouse. I put my feet onto the dirt path and stood, looking up at the constellations, unable to identify anything but the big dipper. The skin of my feet felt cold, but the earth was soft and comforting. I spread my toes and dug them into the ground.

Don't just stand there, start walking, her voice echoed around my head, a little mean, a little judgmental as it often came out. Or was it my own voice? Judgment reflects itself back and forth, a mirror facing a mirror so there are infinite reflections. But walking seemed like a good idea. I grabbed a hoodie and walked down the hill, shoeless, toward the community.

The smell of bonfire smoke hit my face before I saw the fire. I love how the smell of burning wood smoke clings to my clothes, hair, skin. After I've been around a fire, I go as long as I can without bathing to keep the smell embedded, nature's perfume. Two women were sitting around the fire, a young blonde who looked to be my age and an older woman with messy brown hair. They welcomed me to sit with them, knowing who I was. The blonde introduced herself as Jenny. She had a thick German accent.

I'm Angeline, the brunette said.

You must be the New Zealander, I said.

Very good. Most people think I'm Australian when they hear my accent.

Joseph told me there was a New Zealander here.

Of course. What keeps you up at this hour? Angeline said.

I couldn't sleep, I said.

The spirits dance around all night here. It happens to all of us, Jenny said.

I'm traveling with one in particular, I said.

We all have one or two that are closer, but the web ties us all together, Angeline said. Who is she?

I didn't ask how Angeline knew the pronoun of my ghost. The fire popped and silhouetted us in shadows and curling smoke. Maybe we're all ghosts, see-through in the right light. I didn't answer, just kept my eyes on the fire. Jenny reached into a cooler and popped the top off a bottle of beer with a lighter. She extended the beer to me, and said, Prost!

Le'chaim, I said, taking the beer and holding it up. How'd you do that with the lighter?

You're lucky I'm ready for another. I'll show you, Jenny said.

She grabbed another beer and nestled the lighter in the crook of her index finger, positioning it under the bottle cap.

Then you put your thumb underneath, like this, for leverage, and flip it open, she said.

The cap flew off with a satisfying pop and I was impressed for the second time. Angeline was ready for her next one too, so she handed it to me with a nod. I positioned the lighter as instructed and pressed. I managed to ease a corner of the cap off, creating a sad fizzle and a sharp bend around its teeth. We all laughed and they promised I'd get it with a few more rounds of practice.

We have a hot tub here, Jenny said. It's an old horse trough that we built into straw bale and clay, with a space underneath for a fire. It takes about an hour to heat up. We can spark it up tomorrow. For now, we drink and smoke!

Jenny handed me a tin of Drum rolling tobacco after pulling a paper and a pinch of tobacco for herself. I did the same, then passed it to Angeline. We rolled our cigarettes and sat in silence, looking up at the constellations tangled in rising bonfire and tobacco smoke.

16.

She held up a half-smoked Vagina Slime. We were sitting at the old plywood table in her kitchen picking through the ashtray, blowing smoke rings, trying to impress each other, laughing. She blew a ring, then another ring through it. I watched her lips making a perfect O shape, bigger and smaller, big O little o. I showed her how to French inhale, extending my lower jaw causing the smoke to rise then inhaling, a reverse waterfall of smoke from mouth to nostrils. Gross, she said but did it anyway with success on the first try. She was good at everything.

When she was thirteen, she lost her virginity to her also thirteen-year-old boyfriend, who lived with his mom and stepdad in an old brick apartment building like hers, a few blocks away. We smoked cigarettes inside her boyfriend's apartment in front of his mom, sometimes with her, and when she was asleep, he would steal her weed. His mom was always smoking something, never minding what we smoked or that we were smoking in her house. They had sleepovers with the door closed. His mom supplied them with condoms.

She developed early, like her older sisters. They were tough and cool and talked about sex and the intricacies of romance. That first time she and her boyfriend had sex, they were kissing standing up and, still kissing, walked to the bed.

Like in the movies, she said.

She thought it was romantic. I was jealous. Of her, of her boyfriend, of not being either one of them.

17.

The next morning, I found Claudia, Joseph, and Liam in the main house having a breakfast of toast and jam. They invited me to join them at the table. Joseph said I could spend the day working with him on the tree farm pulling weeds, or I could go for a walk through the woods.

Your help is appreciated, but there's no pressure, he said. We just like to host travelers and meet new people. Please do as you like.

I was exhausted from the early mornings and long workdays at Farmer Frank's, happy to be on a freer schedule. I decided to go on a walk and told Joseph I'd work on the tree farm the next day.

I headed down the hill and back, into the woods. The path was marked with a small wooden sign that read, this way, and a red arrow. I started to walk, listening to the crunch of leaves under my feet and the trees swishing in the wind. The air was warm and earthy. I breathed with the wind. I was alone. Again.

After a half an hour of walking, I could see the end of the path where the light opened back up into a big sky and a massive oak tree. The oak's branches were long reaching, each the size and width of the individual trees in the forest I had just come out of.

Its own ecosystem.

Its own entity, older than I would ever be.

As I approached, a shadow cast from above a low branch. I looked up. The sun shone behind her, her silhouette see-through and muted. Only the blue of her eyes. And the feeling of comfort and anxiety, together.

18.

After a few years of being disconnected, she moved into a group house where I had lived for a semester in college, into the room I was leaving to go travel for the summer. She reached out, I responded. It was good to see her in the space between my leaving and her arriving. Time doesn't always heal or change things, but it often softens the harsh light. We knew we'd see each other again that fall.

When I came back for school, she'd had enough of communal living and wanted her own place, but neither of us could afford living alone. We agreed to share a small one-bedroom apartment in walking distance from everywhere we needed to be, and take turns sleeping in the bedroom. We talked about getting a hammock or a blow-up mattress for the floor. We never did. We shared the bed most nights, or one of us slept on the shitty, brown couch we found on the curb, which we named Brownie Turd. We listened to riot grrrl rock and she hung wild crafted herbs around the apartment to dry. She mixed tinctures and boiled herbs to make teas for menstrual cramps, a stuffy nose, a lonely heart. She borrowed my hoodies and I wore her striped tank tops. We fit into each other's clothes and into each other's empty pockets. We filled the gaps with new music, shiny lip rings, and punk rock ideas, picking back up where we left off from our teenage years. I couldn't remember why we parted ways.

The first time we kissed, not on LSD, was later than it should've been. It was pressing behind us, around us, into us. But we ignored it—for fear or avoidance or not wanting to be messy—

until it would no longer be ignored. Our magnets were pulling at each other, but my caution rose up, protective. I was afraid. Not of the darkness. The darkness was what drew me in. But of something else. Something I couldn't isolate. Something I couldn't say out loud.

It happened on the brown curb Brownie Turd couch with a boy she liked. He came over to take staged photographs of us in old lingerie, like Cindy Sherman character studies. I didn't know who Cindy Sherman was. We took turns lying on the couch in a tattered beige camisole, one arm overhead, looking vacant. I felt stupid, knowing the camera didn't love me and that this was about how beautiful she was. At the end of the shoot, we squeezed onto the couch with a case of cheap beer. They kissed, he kissed me, I kissed her, we all kissed. Our eyes synced together, their eyes, then our eyes again. The tension relieved. Or at least, one of the tensions. When I was satisfied enough and too drunk-tired to keep going, I went to sleep in the bed and they squeezed together on the couch. We didn't talk about any of it. He continued coming around for several weeks after that, but I was never invited back in and didn't ask to be. I didn't want them both. I just wanted her. She wanted him and he clearly wanted her back. But by the next month, he was gone. He did something stupid and she was mad. He was gone, having annoyed her more than she was willing to put up with, and I was glad. He tried to call and come back around, but she grew icy the way she did and he didn't know how to make her ice melt. He turned to me. But how do you help someone stay when you want them to leave? I wanted her to myself.

For a few months, we loved each other part time, mostly in our shared bed at night and at parties on the weekends. We never called ourselves anything, the unnamed caution never thinning. But we loved the best we could, awkward and ugly and crying and beautiful. I felt her love in moments, conditional as it was, though taking the moments of tender depth as if they were endless, and reciprocating. I wasn't keen to her extreme variety of hot cold on off. But also, love as we are taught, as we think we know it, has boundaries and edges. Everyone has conditions. Some love sustains, long legato until the story ends. Other love staccatos in and out, forever.

In a moment of out, things went too far outside the edge and began to crumble too much to piece back together. Our youth stunted our ability to communicate the wildness of our hearts. We broke each other, and then, we were too broken. We stayed in the apartment because we had a lease and minimal money and school to finish. We found an unvoiced schedule to give each other space in the smallness of our physicality, and when the semester and the lease ended, we moved to opposite ends of the country, parting again, re-estranged.

19.

I climbed up the tree and sat on the branch in front of her. She took a drag off the cigarette hanging from her mouth, then exhaled the smoke into my face. I opened my mouth and took in her smoke, sucked in like sipping through a straw. We used to call this shotgunning. The intimacy of almost kissing, face up close, tangled eyes and breath. Her mouth closed in on mine as I pulled in air and smoke. First her mouth, then her face, head, torso, and feet. I felt the vibration of her soprano laugh move through my veins like blood and energy, like life. Bodies aren't the only way to be alive. I pulled her smoke, that mirage, those particles of existence, her aliveness into my body. I held her in my lungs for a long time. Too long.

One year after we parted for the second time, her first letter arrived. A handmade envelope covered in pencil sketches of wildflowers. Inside, thin paper with small, delicate words of apologies and love.

Accountability.

Hindsight.

Regret.

A voice I'd never heard. She had moved in with her dad in Virginia, into the house he built after her parents split up. She started going to therapy. She was finding stillness. She learned how to play the banjo. She wanted to come to the west coast for a visit.

I read the letter ten times and each time I read, I cried. I immediately wrote her back, absolved and accepting all of it. My heart broke open hard, one clean crack, no struggle, no scattered shards. I told her to come visit. I told her I loved her. I told her we could start again. The past is its own story. It tangles, but its threads are loose and nimble. We don't need it to be where we are.

A few weeks later, the next letter came. I knew it was hers as soon as I touched it, an envelope made from an old map of California and her small, perfect penmanship. She wrote more about the banjo, making herbal medicines, the Virginia landscape, the growth of her relationship with her father. I wrote about my own life, the way friends tell each other things, easy without eggshells or breaking glass. Our words became tender and our feelings, woven. We wrote back and forth. She sent more drawings of plants and hopefulness. I started to think she would actually come for a visit. I wanted her to. I wanted to squeeze her body and feel her body squeeze mine, her laugh too loud in my face, her eyes piercing but soft in my eyes. I was ready. We started making plans. I sent a letter suggesting a month in the fall for a visit. I sent my new phone number, told her to call and we could set a date. And then, I waited.

A letter from coast to coast takes less than a week. But then there's receiving it, carving time and space to sit in bed or next to a window or under a tree with a cup of tea or a glass of wine, to read slowly and take it all in. Then the rereading, thinking about what you want to say, what the other person meant, answering all the questions and responding to all the ideas. Drawing pictures, finding the perfect envelope, the perfect stamp, the perfect way to write someone's name. I waited, at first without waiting. After a few weeks I started waiting with more eagerness, waiting with waiting, thinking, remembering, wondering.

Waiting.

One month, then two, three, four.

At some point, all at once really, like a switch that goes from on to off, up to down, one click, I realized there would be no more letters.

Maybe she was overwhelmed.

Maybe she was done with me.
Hot cold on off. Click.
She never came to visit. And then, her father called.

20.

I passed through the community on my way back from the woods. Jenny called out to me from her cabin. We sparked up the hot tub. It should be ready to go any minute. Come join, she said.

I'll just grab a towel from the yurt, I said.

When I returned, Jenny and Angeline were already submerged. The tub was made from a long, metal horse trough, comfortably fitting five adult bodies side by side. A roaring fire blazed beneath, like a giant pot on a stove boiling the people. Human stew. I got in next to Jenny and she handed me an unopened beer and a lighter.

Let's see what you can do, she said, laughing.

I placed the lighter under the cap, positioned my fingers, took a breath, and gave it everything I had. With a pop and a fizz, the cap flew off into the grass below. Everyone cheered. I felt satisfied.

What's all the commotion? Claudia said. She and Liam arrived with their own towels.

Angeline reached for Liam, picking up his tiny body and dunking him into the hot water. I told Claudia about the new trick I learned. She told me she had just mastered it herself. Liam yelled and splashed and Claudia warned him that they'd leave if he didn't calm down. We all laughed, even Claudia. She asked about my walk in the woods.

I found a huge oak tree, I said.

At the end of the trail? Angeline asked.

I nodded.

I saw my father there once. After he died, Claudia said.

There's an old woman who lives at the very top, Jenny said.

You saw her there, didn't you? Your ghost? Angeline said.

I nodded again. They all looked at me, waiting for me to say something. I took a big gulp of beer.

She's following me, I said.

I didn't want to sound scared or sad because I didn't feel either of those. I didn't feel anything. They waited, I shrugged and drank more beer. I wanted to talk about her, but also, I didn't know where to start or how much to say surrounded by familiar strangers. The past needs to feel acknowledged in order to unclench its fists. But the timing of time is so fussy. Another beer gulp.

The woman, Jenny said, sometimes doesn't look old. You know that picture that looks like either an old woman or a young girl, depending on how your brain translates the lines? She's like that. It depends on the light and the angles, and mostly, how I feel when I see her. And maybe how she feels when she arrives.

I looked at Jenny, her eyes glossy from the heat and the feeling of seeing something inside the emotion of memory.

I said, She was the young girl in the picture. Made of inky lines on paper. But in every other way, she was the old woman who knows things. Too many things. You know, unintentional self-imposed madness.

Everything is self-imposed, isn't it? Angeline said.

Even ghosts, Claudia said.

I dreamed I got a postcard from a man I had never met. I'd heard of him, but the connection was fuzzy. The postcard had a collage of hand drawn plant sketches, their Latin names scribbled in cursive:

Opium poppy, Papaver samniferum.

English lavender, Lavandula angustifolia.

Marigold, Calendula officinalis.

Purple coneflower, Echinacea purpurea.

Starflower, Borage officinalis

The cursive letters erased when I touched them, then reappeared when I moved my hand away. On the back of the postcard was a mirror, but it was her face reflected back to me. I turned the card back over and found it postmarked London, signed Daniel. I thought about the dream when I woke up, a feeling of knowing something I didn't know. What was I supposed to know? And then, I remembered who he was. An old friend of hers, somehow important. We'd never met, but she always said someday we would.

I got dressed and walked down the hill to Angeline's airstream. She invited me in, made coffee, and I told her about the dream.

Strange, she said. But not that strange.

What do you mean?

The lines are thinner than you think, she said.

I was quiet. She continued.

No matter how far away you think you are, there is always a thread that keeps you tied to the web, she smiled.

I sipped my coffee and nodded.

She said, You get to choose whether or not to listen. Dismissal is an option. But listening is much more fun.

Maybe I should go to London, I said.

I'd say so.

I spent the next day pulling weeds around Joseph's tiny Christmas trees. Wind rustled, pigeons cooed, and a bird sang a song that sounded like a schoolyard bully making fun of someone. I heard her laugh inside the mean bird song. Her laugh made me laugh. She wanted me to go to London to see her friend. I listened. I knew without knowing how I knew, without logic. But my guts knew, which were becoming a much more trustworthy source than my linear mind.

That night, we all went to a local pub in town. I was excited for the distraction. Listen, and then forget everything you hear.

They're playing traditional Irish music tonight, Joseph said.

The pub was dark and dreamy and full of singing and dancing. I sat at the bar, and before I could order, the bartender lined up three stouts in front of me.

Guinness, Murphy's, O'Hara's, he said, pointing to each as he named them.

I didn't order these, I said.

He laughed and said, These are from all of us. Enjoy.

He waved an arm around the bar and said, We know you're not from here—this is our hospitality. It's a meal in a can. Or three meals. You'll have to drink them all.

He winked and laughed.

I thanked him and turned to thank the bar. Everyone cheered and I held up the Guinness, taking a big, creamy gulp.

As the night progressed, the music grew louder, the dancing more vibrant, and the flow of beer, bottomless. I was pulled up to dance by red-nosed drunk people I had never met, then tossed toward my friends who swung me around by the elbow and laughed. Joy arrived in waves and bursts. I forgot to remember the strangeness of the world and the separation between worlds. Everything was happening at once without time, stillness and movement synced together.

Bird songs at night.

A crescent moon view at noon.

Waves heaving through a creek.

Truth shows its two-way mirror as soon as you forget to recall. Drinking helps too. Letting go, getting free. There were times I also wanted to disappear, like I knew she did, to stop the seesaw. But it was never for lack of care of others. We are all in the center of our own bubbles, see-through as they may be. If you're not centered, you're disembodied. And if you don't see out, you're stuck. The point isn't one extreme or the other, but to find balance. I was never angry about her choice because choice is all we have and all we can hope for.

Joseph helped me book a cheap flight to London through Ryanair. I said goodbye to the community and told them I'd be back someday. I didn't know if that was true, but I wanted it to be. He drove me to the Cork airport, where I boarded a tiny plane and headed back to England.

21.

I wasn't sure how to find Daniel. What I remembered was a café. Vauxhall. I had started putting the memories together. London is not a place to go without ground. But my guidebook helped me secure a cheap hostel for a few nights while I searched. I asked the young rocker girl at the front desk about Vauxhall cafés and gay bars. She pulled an old receipt out of her bag and drew me a map of all the places worth visiting.

Something with Vauxhall in the name, I said.

There are a few. Go here first.

Then she said, what or who are you looking for?

Someone I haven't met yet.

Well, that'll be interesting.

Do you happen to know someone named Daniel who works at one of these places?

She laughed, which led me to believe she didn't. Then she said, Sorry no. But good luck then.

The street was lined in billowing rainbow flags. I picked the first café on the list and walked right up to the girl at the counter. I asked her if there was ever someone named Daniel who had worked there. She said no. Her nametag read Gaal, which means wave in Hebrew. I asked her if she was Israeli.

In fact I am, she said.

At medaberit ivrit? I asked.

Bevadai, she said.

I smiled and she smiled back. Her sparkly eyes catching all the rainbows. I told her my story.

She said, Well I don't know Daniel, but I think I can help you find him. Would you have a drink with me later?

Gaal was taller than me, but only by a few inches. Her nostrils were big and perfect on a slick nose. I love a good nose. We met at one of the bars on my list. She was already there when I arrived, wearing a Misfits T-shirt with the sleeves cut off and raggedy jean shorts, sitting at the bar talking to the bartender. I was impressed with her shirt.

I ordered you a gin and tonic, local London gin. Is that okay? She said.

That's my favorite, thanks.

We clinked our glasses and she pointed to the bartender and said, This is Phil and he knows everyone. Maybe he can help you find your Daniel?

Phil and I shook hands. He said, I might know the person you're looking for. What's he look like?

I saw of picture of him once, I said. What I remember was that he had shaggy brown hair and a tattoo of a poppy flower on his forearm. I think he worked around here somewhere.

Phil looked over at the other bartender. She was vigorously shaking a drink. I followed his eyes to her shaking forearm. When the shaking stopped, I saw the poppy tattoo.

Dee, he yelled to her and motioned for her to come over.

She served the drink and came to where Gaal and I were sitting. The tattoo was familiar. It was the one in the picture. I was sure. I introduced myself and asked her if she knew who I was. Her marble hazel eyes locked into mine.

She said, Well of course I do honey.

I stayed with Gaal until the bar closed. We spoke in Hebrew and English, back and forth, secretly talking about people around us in Hebrew when we didn't want them to know what we were saying. She told me I was beautiful. I told her she was hot. She leaned in to kiss me smelling of gin and limes, boozy citrus breath. I kissed her back.

Let's go to my flat, she said.

Yes. But I have to talk to Dee.

Of course. We'll meet her for brunch tomorrow. I arranged it when you were in the bathroom.

That night, I slept with Gaal in her crappy but comfortable futon. I dreamed the poppy tattoo on Dee's forearm was growing up her neck changing color, orange, blue, purple, silver. In the dream, Dee's voice was her voice. She said, You finally made it. Smell the flowers. I leaned into the tattoo and breathed in lavender and coffee. I kissed the ink, the skin on Dee's arm, her neck then her lips. Her laugh arrived loud between my temples. So loud it woke me suddenly and too early, just as the sun was coming up. Gaal was still deep in a dream that, according to her smile, seemed euphoric. I got out of bed, careful not to ruffle the blankets, and stepped out onto the balcony. I watched the city begin to stir, people in suits and high heel shoes shuffling around each other trying not to spill their to-go coffee cups, taxis swerving too fast around parked cars and people in crosswalks, pigeons cooing on balconies, the morning light perfectly casting shadows. I breathed in and held my breath as long as I could.

22.

I want a poppy tattoo like this, she said.

She handed me a picture of Daniel.

Then she lifted her shirt exposing her right side and said, but mine will go all the way up, hip to armpit.

We had already gotten tattooed together a few months earlier. A tattoo artist friend of a friend was traveling through town trying to make extra cash, working out of the friend's basement. He had a good reputation and reasonable prices. The artist was young and confident with bright green eyes and covered in his own tattoos.

Never get tattooed from someone who doesn't have tattoos.

She was in an upswing, flirty and charming. I wanted her to feel good. When she felt good, things were easy. But the nexus of their eyes, blue green blue green, was strong and locked in. I was jealous. I wrapped my feelings tight inside my guts, a weighted blanket fort around my chest.

Don't rock the dinghy.

Smile and nod.

Be cool.

We showed him our drawings, and he told her how cool hers was. Flirting and flirting. Her tattoo was a snake wrapped around a small basket of eggs on the scar on her belly, where that ovary was removed. It wasn't cancer. It just wasn't functional. Dead ovary. If we don't take it out it can cause problems later, they said. She hated the scar, even when I told her it was beautiful.

Look how it creases when I bend forward, she whined, twisting her face.

She rarely whined. The scar was the only instigator. We all have something.

My tattoo was an Aries symbol on my back, curved thick lines around my shoulders and filled in black. We had been working on our tattoo drawings for a couple of weeks, showing each other our pictures and helping each other revise.

She wanted to go first. The artist set up a massage table and told her to lie down, pull up her shirt, and unbutton her pants. She reached for my hand. I sat beside the table while she breathed deep and occasionally laughed as the sting of tattoo needles stabbed her skin. Hers would hurt more than mine, I was sure. The tenderness of belly flesh. But she didn't flinch with pain, never squeezed her eyes or puckered her mouth or swore. Her pain wasn't physical.

After hers and after mine, he asked for her number. Our number. He called the next day. She met him at a bar, then spent the night back in the tattoo basement with him. When she came home, she asked what I thought of him. She beamed, blushing and smiling.

He's fine, I said.

Just fine?

Fine.

Isn't he so cute? She said.

He's fine, I said.

She rolled the blue of her eyes, up and back. My opinion mattered even though it didn't feel like it mattered. He called again, but before they could meet, he went back to Vegas and that was the end of it. I could feel her sadness, and also, I was glad he was gone, knowing the weight of her love would shift back toward me. I wasn't at the front of her line, but that wasn't a responsibility I wanted anyway.

When the tattoos healed, she was ready for her next one. That's when she showed me the picture of Daniel's poppies.

I want flowers too, I said.

We talked about our plants. We drew pictures. We showed each other and revised again, and then again, things fell apart.

The apex where all the lines of goodness cross.

The coming down from the going up.

The stick in the spoke of the bike wheel.

We only got tattooed together once.

23.

Gaal made Turkish coffee. Café botz, mud coffee, from Israel. I was tempted to drink a cup, the smell of cardamom familiar and comforting, but I knew I'd have coffee at brunch and didn't want to be jittery. I wanted to be calm with Dee, to let the circumstance hold its heft. Death changes a person's story, like a choose-your-own-adventure twist of outcomes. Ghosts live novels, linear narratives that don't exist for the living. We can see the past as parts that fit together, because the future, and even the present, no longer sustain.

Dee was sitting on the patio at the café when we arrived, sipping a latté. She waved at us, smiling and warm. We exchanged cheek kisses, small talk, and ordered coffee and a brunch of eggs, beans, toast, and potatoes. When the food arrived, Dee started talking.

I had a dream about you, she said.

I had a dream about you too, I said.

Well well, isn't our old ghost busy, she said.

I shrugged, and Dee and Gaal laughed.

She really loved you, Dee said. She was afraid to send the letters. She thought you were done with her.

I know, I said. I loved her too. I loved her letters.

Well that's what I told her. You know, she had an attempt after the ovary surgery. I found her.

I didn't know that.

She had all those pain meds. But I don't think she was really serious then. She wasn't ready.

So that's why she didn't want the meds after she got her wisdom teeth out, I said.

Dee nodded like she already knew. Gaal ate and listened intently.

I said, I picked her up after at the dentist. She was crying hysterically but she couldn't talk. Her mouth was full of cotton. They told me to stop at the pharmacy to pick up the pain meds and when she heard them, she shook her head and looked at me hard, like she was screaming through her eyes, no. The next day, she put together all these herbs she had lying around our apartment. That's all she took. She didn't even take ibuprofen. And I realized it wasn't the pain in her mouth, but the trauma in her heart that made her cry.

Sounds about right, Dee said.

She didn't want those pills around, I said.

She was thorough that way, Dee said.

But she never told me, I said.

Listen, Dee said, she tried. She tried so hard to be okay and at the end, to even be happy. She asked me once, is this it? I feel pretty happy, I think, but is this the best it gets? Like it wasn't enough for her. Like maybe, the temporary feeling of joy was too temporary and too shallow.

I get it, I said.

When I think about her, I don't feel angry that she chose to bail. I'm only mad that she never got out here to visit me, Dee said.

I'm not angry either, I said.

Of everyone I ever knew, Dee said, she never judged me and she didn't flinch when I came out to her. She said, you're you, whatever your name is, whatever your body is. Just don't be a dick and I'll always love you. My parents, my family, my old friends, none of them ever said anything like that to me. Even in her darkness, she didn't use my tenderness against me.

I wanted to tell Dee it was different for me. But also, I wanted to stay in the warmth of remembering. Memory is curated. We can choose where it goes. It's the difference between reaction and response. I wanted to hear about Dee's experience, and also to absorb it, feel it intrinsically. Not bouncing off, but sewing together. I didn't ask what she meant about darkness, or how it came out. Maybe I knew. Maybe I wanted to move forward instead of sinking down.

I half smiled at Dee. She full smiled back, leaned in, took my hand and said, Why don't you stay with me for a few days.

Dee lived above a bakery on the rainbow flag street. Her apartment was open and airy, white curtains billowing in the breeze. One of the walls was covered floor to ceiling in photographs of people at pride parades, panoramas and close ups of faces kissing, smiling, crying, and laughing.

Make yourself at home, Dee said.

I always wondered what these apartments looked like, Gaal said, peeking around all the corners. This building is so old, she said.

It's historic, Dee said. Full of ghosts.

I stood in front of the photograph wall and my eyes landed on the picture.

You have a picture of me, I said.

It was a good moment. Not a false good moment, like, smile for the picture, but a real one. She was wearing my striped tank top, which I eventually let her keep, and I had one of her scarves wrapped around my head. She had just bleached my hair and it was a mess. Black hair does not bleach well at home. I didn't care. I shaved my head all the time back then. We weren't trying to look pretty. We wanted to be tough and weird and wild. I heard her laughing, saw her face move, her eyes sparkling in the photograph.

She sent me that one years ago, Dee said. Her eyes follow you like Mona Lisa.

I took a deep breath, almond croissant and roasted coconut.

It smells so good here, I said.

It's the bakery below. Want something? They give me freebies.

I felt Gaal's hand on my shoulder. I was still looking at the picture.

I do! she said to Dee. Then to me, That's her?

I nodded.

How beautiful, she said. Her eyes.

That night I slept on Dee's fold out couch adjacent to the wall of photos. Gaal went back to her apartment. We made a plan to meet up the next evening when she got off work. Dee made up the bed for me with a plush down comforter and two fluffy pillows. Everything in her apartment was perfect, clean, and beautiful. Curated. I lay in bed, cocooned and warm and awake.

She was looming.

The heat of the photograph, pulsing.

Ghosts use material objects to have presence with the living. This may or may not be true. But truth is relative. I saw her in the picture. I saw her see me. As the room grew dark, the moon rose until it beamed in through the window above my bed. I watched its light move, methodical across the wall, each photograph in its diagonal path temporarily illuminated. A spotlight in the art gallery. When the moonbeam landed on us, my own eyes reflected its shine, but her face stayed encased in shadow.

Shadows always moving.

My body sinking into gravity.

And the shadows, as they do at night, coming to life.

I slept. Then I woke. The room was darker now as the moon was long gone, fully risen. I heard her in the bathroom. It was Dee. She was throwing up. I listened for a while to make sure, then got up and knocked on the bathroom door.

Are you okay? I asked.

Could you get me a glass of water?

I ran to the kitchen. When I came back, the bathroom door was open and she was washing her face. I handed her the water.

Thanks honey. It's probably just nerves. Go back to bed, she said.

She touched my arm and I touched her hand and smiled.

Ok, I said. Goodnight.

I went back to the fluffy couch and fell into a deep sleep. Finally. When I woke again, dreamless and disoriented, Gaal was knocking on the door.

I swapped days with someone so I'm free today, she said. Then, Your hair looks wild.

I touched my head and laughed and got back into the comforter cocoon. She put on the water for coffee and got into the cocoon with me. We pulled our heads under the covers. The light glowed through the whiteness of the blanket. She smiled big and I kissed her until the kettle whistled.

Coffee time! she said.

Dee came out of her room as Gaal was plunging the French press. She poured three cups and we all sat together on the fold out bed, drinking and nibbling almond croissants from the bakery downstairs. I asked Dee how she was feeling.

Better, she said with a weak smile.

I touched her hand.

Grief manifests itself in our fragile spots, Dee said.

Gaal took a big croissant bite, crumbs scattering over my legs. I gave her a dirty look. We all laughed. Her eyes lit up and she said, Have you been to France?

Only for a second. I flew into Paris, I said.

No fuck Paris, she said. I mean the south. I hate my job and was thinking about quitting. Let's go!

I'd heard the south of France was the most beautiful place. I wanted to go. I wanted to go everywhere, to keep moving. If you stay somewhere too long, things get messy. Gaal said we could take the cheap bus through the tunnel to Paris and from there, hitch south. I wouldn't have chosen to go back to France. But Gaal made everything sound good. Even the tunnel, which I hadn't yet realized was not just underground, but under water.

24.

I gave Dee my address and wrote hers down in my notebook. I promised to write. I had a feeling she would be a good pen pal, and I wanted to stay in touch, to keep our common thread alive.

We kissed cheeks and she said, You can come back if things don't work out. You know what I mean. She winked.

I felt connected to her in a way I hadn't felt with anyone in a long time. We were only separated by one degree. I breathe out, you breathe in, she breathes out, I breathe in. Our threads are deeply woven. All the cellular, visceral ways we know each other, even when we don't know we know. Dee was the hardest to leave and the easiest to remember.

The bus station smelled like piss and cigarettes and was full of people who didn't seem to notice anyone else was around. Disgusting, in a good way. I was happy to have a travel companion, to have someone else watching my back, my stuff, my heart. The bus ride was long and as we approached the tunnel halfway in, I realized there was water between England and France. The realization hit me in a sudden wave of panic.

Of course, Gaal said. We go under the water. There's no other way, but don't worry they do it all the time. Just close your eyes.

She took my hand and I squeezed my eyes shut hard, trying not to think about a bus moving inside a tunnel somehow built through water. The New York City subway is like this too, and it also makes me panic. If the New York subway stopped being maintained by humans, it would flood with water within days. But a bus is even more vulnerable than a train. Trains are faster and less susceptible to error. Is that true? I don't know, but in that moment I thought so. I thought about all the possible terrible outcomes of humanity trying to manipulate nature in order to move, to have things, to be comfortable, the disconnect of who we are in relation to where we come from. Gaal held my hand and smiled a reassuring smile at me, then put her head on my shoulder and fell asleep. Her snoring was annoying, but her nostrils perfect in profile. My eyes wouldn't stay closed.

I felt the darkness.

I smelled the cigarette smoke.

Virginia Slim vagina slime.

I was moving in an attempt to be free. But freedom has nothing to do with movement. The bus lights were dim inside, most of the passengers sleeping. I eased Gaal's head off my shoulder, careful not to wake her, and took a walk up and down the aisle to stretch my legs. The seat at the front of the bus was empty. I sat. The driver looked at me in the oversized rear view mirror and smiled.

Long trip, I said. Must be hard to drive.

You get used to it, he said.

I looked out the windshield, trying to see what he saw, headlights and shadows passing in streaks. My eyes hurt.

Lots of time to think, he said.

Lots to think about, I said.

He nodded, his gaze steady on the road.

I stood again and turned to walk back toward our seats, close to the back of the bus. She was standing in front of the rear window, cigarette smoke curling around her face from the Virginia Slim hanging from her mouth. Her eyes reflected each headlight that passed and shone through the windows. Icy blue. She looked angry.

What are you doing? She said.

What?

I said, What are you doing? She articulated the "t" in what and the "g" in doing.

What are you doing? I said.

She took a drag off the cigarette.

You're the one that left, I said.

I wasn't angry, but I was starting to feel exhausted. Forgetting to remember wove her in tighter. I meant for it to loosen the knots. Or, I didn't mean to do anything at all.

Another drag.

Deep in, held in, all the way in.

She blew the smoke out in one forceful puff toward my face, the space around my body encased in smoke. I coughed and waved my hand around my face. When the smoke cleared, she was gone.

Hey, what are you doing? Come sit down, Gaal yell whispered to me.

I was just stretching my legs, I said.

I sat back in my seat beside her.

You look pale. Are you still scared of the water tunnel? I think we're already through it.

No I'm okay, I fake smiled.

Let's eat some baguette and cheese, she said.

She reached between her feet and ripped a chunk of bread out of her bag. I took a big bite, chewing for a long time, the way they tell you to get your saliva really involved with your food, to chew until the food is eviscerated, the sensation of dry bread turning to liquid in my mouth. Gaal ate quickly like a hungry animal, tearing and wild. I liked watching her eat. Wildness is sexy. She looked me in the eye and ripped into the bread, crumbs spraying around her face.

I laughed.

What? she said even though she knew why I was laughing. She laughed back, then looked out the window. I followed her gaze.

The sky was starting to lighten, moving us into the next day. Daylight is a relief.

We didn't stay in Paris. I never stayed in Paris. We took a city bus that got us to the edge of town, into the south suburbs where the streets were quieter and the wind blew easy. Gaal stuck her thumb out. I sat on our bags. I was tired. And I wanted to keep going. Tired, going, going, tired. Resting is an easy gift you don't know you need.

A small red sports car, low to the ground and cramped, pulled over and Gaal ran toward it. I walked, big breath in, long breath out. I wanted to keep going. I wanted to go. I did. I didn't. I did. The driver rolled down the passenger window, dance music spilling out. He bopped his head up and down with the bass and pulled his mirrored sunglasses to the tip of his nose. Gaal stuck her head in. She spoke in broken French. I let her take the lead. She told him we were headed to Montpellier. He said he could take us just outside of Bourges, a couple hours south, which would get us about a third of the way to our destination. We got in, Gaal up front, me squeezed in back with our bags. I closed my eyes. He offered us cigarettes and bottles of water. The gifts of France. Offering without strings is impetus. The guy didn't seem creepy, just a fast driver, young and careless. I welcomed time alone in the back seat encased in booming music and language barrier. I fell into a deep, vibrational sleep.

We decided to find a cheap hotel in Bourges, to eat and get a good night of rest. The historical town was covered in quaint shops and stone paved streets, magical. Gaal was a bottomless pit of energy, excited and ready for everything. She slept effortlessly and woke refreshed. I envied her ease and also, it grated me.

Tomorrow, she said, we'll make it all the way to Montpellier in one ride. I have a feeling.

My internal dialogue pressed around my guts.

Stay positive.

Be cool.

The next day on our walk to the edge of town, we stopped at a café to order two chocolate croissants and un petit café. Chocolate and butter for breakfast. I stuck my thumb out, leaning into Gaal's body, feeling vibrant and jacked from the strong coffee. The air was perfect, a cool breeze blowing our hair around each other's faces. We waited for an hour. She didn't complain. I complained in my head, but never out loud. Waiting comes when you need it.

One ride to Montpellier. Watch. I'm telling you, she said.

I believe you, I said.

I did. I didn't. I did. I believed her words and her beautiful guts. I decided her truth would be true, that if we both believed it, it had energy to happen.

An old mint green Datsun pulled up with a smiling pit bull face hanging out the passenger window. The driver looked to be in her late thirties. She had a messy ponytail, dirty jeans, and a torn Pixies T-shirt. Her eyes, Mediterranean Sea turquoise blue.

Her eyes follow me wherever I go.

Her eyes follow you like Mona Lisa.

Bonjour où allez-vous? the driver said.

Gaal told her we were trying to get to Montpellier.

Ah you speak English? she said.

Gaal nodded.

She smiled and said, I'm Margot. This is Claude. Yes, I will take you to the sea. Come in.

Gaal looked at me, her eyes wider than her smile, her nostrils in a joyful flare. I told you, she said.

You did, I said.

We threw our bags into the pick-up bed and scooted in next to Claude, who promptly sat on my lap and licked my face.

He's very nice, Margot said.

I love animals, I said.

Yes, I can see. He knows too, she said.

Merci beaucoup, Gaal said to Margot.

Of course. It's better to drive with other people, Margot said.

She offered us chocolate and cigarettes. Safety. A PJ Harvey tape playing:

Tie yourself to me / no one else
No you're not rid of me / you're not rid of me

I love this song, Gaal said, which made me like her a little less. I loved the song too. I love PJ Harvey. But it wasn't a song for the moment. It was from the past, nostalgic and full of punches. I wanted to turn the volume all the way up and scream:

I beg you, my darling / don't leave me, I'm hurting
Lick my legs, I'm on fire
Lick my legs of desire

I looked down at Claude on my lap. His eyes in my eyes. Animals know everything without knowing they know. I wanted to cry. I didn't. But Claude could see. He licked my eyes. I kissed him and looked out the window, blowing French cigarette smoke around the passing highway signs.

Can I turn it up? I said.

Of course, Margot said, turning the volume knob.

Margot and Gaal sang. I felt my lungs breathing deep with smoke, relaxing my body. Smoking makes you take deep breaths, part of the reason it's calming. A disgusting delusion.

We drove fast through the French countryside, rolling hills, then suburbs, then more country, mountains, water. The feeling of air blowing in my face was the wind bath I needed. I wanted to keep moving. Start again every day, several times a day. But also, I longed for the comfort of stillness. Repeatedly doing the same thing, even movement, makes an easy groove to get stuck in. Each time you go around, the groove gets deeper, the well, heavier.

Stuckness.

Illusion of freedom.

Margot pulled the truck into a gas station.

It doesn't look like it, but they have a very good pan bagnat sandwich here, she said.

The car doors squeaked when we opened them and Claude jumped out, ready to have a stretch and pee. I felt the same way. Margot pumped gas and Gaal went inside to buy sandwiches.

You are girlfriends? Margot asked me.

I don't know, I said. We just met.

Aha, she smiled. This is the best time. The beginning.

It may not be the beginning of anything.

You have someone else?

Sort of.

Love is complicated, Margot said. But you can always make more love.

Gaal came back with the sandwiches and Claude jumped up, propping his front paws on her thigh. He wagged his tail in hopes of a bite.

Claude couche! Assis. Margot said.

He jumped off her legs and sat.

I kneeled down and told him he was a good boy. He smiled and licked my face. We sat at a small wooden table under a tree behind the gas station and ate our sandwiches. Margot put a bowl of food and water down for Claude. The sun was warm on my face. It felt good to be stopped, to eat, to look at the view. I could be anything, anywhere. Grounded, ungrounded.

I wanted to get to the sea, to be all the way at the edge, at a stopping place. I wanted to throw her into the water and cover her in remedial sea salt. Or maybe I was the one that needed the salt to draw and dry my insides out. Osmosis. I never wanted to grow anything in my body. She was afraid her body wouldn't make a baby after the ovary was removed.

Who cares, I said.

I care bitch, she said.

Sorry, I said. Sorry.

And then, when I thought I was doing the carrying, she carried me.

25.

She stood at the sink facing away from the toilet.

Okay I'm done, I said. You can turn around.

I felt my eyes fill with water and my throat start to close.

It'll be okay, she said.

The second line appeared on the stick, confirming what I already knew. Crying turned to sobbing.

My cousin went to the clinic last year, she said. It was fine. I'll borrow my mom's car. Don't worry.

She picked me up the following week. As we pulled up to the clinic, people with signs stood outside marching and chanting.

A-holes, she said. Don't they have to go to work or something?

I laughed.

She parked the car and we walked through the protesters. I held my head high. They didn't scare me. In fact, they made me feel strong, the way you ground harder when someone challenges what you know is right. She gave them the middle finger and glared. They called us sinners. Yes, we said, we are proud sinners!

The woman at the desk gave me a clipboard and said someone would be with me soon. I looked around at the other girls in the waiting room, all of us young, some looking panicked. I couldn't wait for it to be over. Not because I was afraid, but because I knew I had made a mistake and this was the way to fix it. No time was the right time for me.

I was called into a room with the other girls. We were told we had many options, that there was still time to make other choices, then asked if we had questions. No one said anything. No questions, no eyes, no feelings. The woman seemed disappointed. She signed and, as she left the room, she told us to read through all the pamphlets and that she'd be back soon. We sat in the room for an hour. Just the sounds of shuffling thick paper opening and closing, knees shaking in anxiety, sneakers tapping the dirty linoleum, sighing. One girl started to cry quietly. I thought she might leave, but she didn't. She just closed her eyes and bowed her head as the tears fell. I stared at the wall with my hands in my lap, shutting it all out. I didn't open any booklets. I didn't look at anyone's eyes. When the woman finally came back, she encouraged us again to ask questions and pressed that we could, should, make different choices. And again, silence.

Ok then follow me, she said.

We walked behind her in a single line into another room. She pointed to a shelf and told us to change into the hospital gowns and put the paper booties on our feet and over our hair. When we were done changing, she led us to a row of chairs where we each took a seat, waiting for our turn. A nurse came by with two choices of meds: one to just numb the pain, or one to knock you out. I chose the first. I wanted to be awake and aware, to feel the change happen in my body, to make sure it was real. I picked up two small paper cups, one with the pill, one with water, and swallowed. As I waited, I watched Vanna White dressed in a long, sparkly gown flip large letters on the TV hanging from the ceiling. The girl next to me started giggling. Her laugh sounded far away, like it was coming from the TV. I looked at her. She looked at me. Our eyes the same eyes. I laughed too, the stoned heaviness of her lids against the lightness of not caring, or forgetting to care.

When my turn came, the nurse walked me into the procedure room and told me to lie on the table and place my feet in the stirrups. She patted my hand. The doctor came in, chipper and smiling and said it would take less than five minutes. I'd hear the sound of a vacuum and a little pinch and then it would be over.

Here we go, he said, like we were about to take a fun boat ride together.

The vacuum started. Then the pinch. Then also, a pull, a tear, and a punch. I squeezed the nurse's hand, not having realized I was holding it in the first place. I squeezed her hand hard, harder, crushing the delicate bones of her thin fingers, the drugs completely worn off. I felt my face get wet with hot tears. I heard my voice, far away crying like the laughing girl sitting next me, like canned laughter on a TV sitcom. Not sad or scared or pain crying. But deep relief crying. Deep relief. The pain not pain, because it meant an end to a beginning that never should have happened.

All done, the doctor said, still chipper. He took his latex gloves off with a pop and left.

The nurse helped me off the table and walked me to a room full of beds. She gave me a huge maxi pad and a belt to hook it onto, those pads they used before pads had adhesive and thinner material was invented in the eighties. A sack stuffed with thick cotton. There's so much blood, you need all that density. She explained I'd need to change the pad every few hours for a few days, until the bleeding stopped.

You can stay here for twenty minutes, then we'll need the bed, she said.

I sipped the concentrated orange juice and ate a few of the saltines they put out on a hospital tray beside the bed. The juice was yellow and reminded me of kindergarten. It made me nauseous. I watched the clock, waiting for nineteen minutes to go by. I wanted to lie down and go to sleep, but I knew I didn't have time for sleep. I knew they'd kick me out and I didn't want to get kicked out. I wanted to leave before they could tell me to go. I wanted to make my own decision.

I hobbled into the waiting room, my bulky pad swishing between my legs like a diaper. She was there, waiting. I looked at her face, her water eyes soft waves on a calm day. I looked at her eyes and I started crying. The comfort of safe vulnerability.

She also carried me.

The nurse gave her a bag with supplies and instructions and she put her arm around me as we walked back out to the car. Over the next week, she brought me food, flowers, water, jokes.

She also carried me.

26.

We arrived in Montpellier as the sun was setting. Margot said she could take us all the way to the beach. She was headed that way anyway.

I'm going to sleep on the beach tonight. You can sleep near me, no one will bother you. Claude will protect us, she said.

She pulled the truck onto a sandy patch and we followed her to an alcove beneath a tree. She laid down a big army tarp and gave us her extra sleeping bag. After we set up camp, we scattered to find sticks around the beach for a fire. The beach was empty, a welcome relief, the stark brink of the world. I took my shoes off and walked to the edge of the water, letting the waves lap my ankles. The coolness of the water soothed my skin and calmed my pulse. I looked out as far as I could, squinting my eyes to find the horizon line. The sky was darkening fast. I felt the faint sounds of Margot, Gaal, and Claude moving somewhere behind me, but didn't turn to look. I watched the waves move forward and back again and again, listening, breathing, feeling. There was nowhere else to be in that moment. The ocean reminds me of how small I am. I stood until the sky was black and I heard them rustling to make a fire. When I smelled the smoke, I walked back to camp.

We sat around the fire warming our hands and feet. Claude, again, on my lap. He was too big, but I let him. Animals are basically all the goodness of people without all the garbage. I fell in love with him so many times. Every time. Margot told us her story:

My lover lives in Barcelona, she said. We have been apart for two months. She was married to a man when we met. She is a painter. I found her work at a gallery in Paris and I knew I had to meet her. Her paintings made me feel free and at home, together. I was so moved looking at the colors, deep blues like the dusk sky, I wanted to cry. It was her art opening, so she was at the gallery. There were so many people but my friend knew her friend, who invited us to stay for the after party that was by invitation only. I saw her through swarms of people. You know how your eyes can shoot through everyone and make a clear path? She was tall and elegant, and wisps of her hair kept falling into her face. She pushed the hair back in this slow and sexy way with her index finger, swirling rosé around a big glass with the other hand. As I watched her, in my mind I said, look at me, look at me, come here. At one point she looked right at me, the same path my eyes took through all the people. She smiled. I looked behind me to make sure she was looking at me. She smiled bigger and laughed. I smiled back. She nodded and then looked back at the people she was talking to. I watched her for a few more minutes, and then I saw her excuse herself and walk toward me. She said to me, you wanted me to come to you, I could feel you. I heard you. So now I'm here. Okay. Who are you? I told her my name and before I could say anything else, she drank the rest of her wine and kissed me. We kissed for a long time. So long that it felt like the world ended.

That night I went to her flat and we made love. I wanted that night to last forever. We stayed awake for as long as we could. When we finally fell asleep, we were wrapped around each other like a puzzle, so that I couldn't tell whose arms were whose. In the morning, she said, go quickly my husband will be home from his work trip soon. I was surprised. But then she said, don't worry I don't love him. I'm going to leave him and go back home to Barcelona soon. As soon as the moment began, it ended. That morning, I thought things were finished, that this was a one-night affair. Her life was too complicated. I knew I didn't want to break up a marriage and I didn't want to make drama. And if she was going to Spain, that would be the end of it. But she stayed in Paris for three more months and we met in secret when her husband was away on business. When he wasn't away, we talked on the phone and still met sometimes. Our secret made our love grow quickly. You know, when you can't have something, you want it more. You give it more. In a way, you let it become so big, the secret stirring around, gaining momentum like a tornado. One night, she called and said she was leaving right away. She had a window to go and she had to take it. She told me to come to Barcelona when I was ready. So now I'm going.

Gaal took my hand. I could feel that she wanted Margot's story to be our story, instant love. I didn't know if Margot felt that kind of love. But I knew I didn't. I knew that I was moving, whether or not I should be moving, whether or not that was the right thing to do. I was moving. And no one was part of my long-term story. Not even my ghost.

I woke up to the sound of chattering seagulls and rolling waves. The sun was just starting to rise. Waves never stop moving, but their rhythm is so steady it feels still. I was spooned with Claude. He seemed to feel my eyes open because as soon as I woke, he stood and wagged his tail, ready for breakfast. Margot and Gaal were still asleep. I whispered to Claude to come with me. We walked to the water. He got in and splashed around while I dipped my feet and threw water on my face.

Come on, I said to him.

We walked along the shore, our toes getting salted and wet. I found a stick and threw it as far as I could. He chased it, caught it, brought it back, and I threw it again and again. Animals are constantly seeking joy. They find it in the simplest places. We walked up and down the beach until the sun was fully up, then headed back to camp. Gaal and Margot were making a new fire.

Well guys I'm going down to Barcelona today, Margot said.

I wanted to go with her. But she didn't invite me, either of us, and I knew I needed more time to be still. We helped her pack up, thanked her for the ride, and cheek kissed. I hugged Claude for too long. I have the hardest time saying goodbye to animals.

He'll miss you, Margot said to me.

I will really miss him, I said.

She smiled.

Au revoir, she said.

Gaal and I found a hostel in town to base out of. We dropped off our bags and spent the morning walking around town drinking coffee and eating baguettes and cheese until we got hot and needed to swim. The hostel had old loaner cruiser bikes, so we borrowed a couple and rode back to the beach. The wind felt good in my hair, which was twisted and tangled from salty seawater. I put my shoes in the basket on the front of the bike as I rode, airing out my feet, my skin, all the parts of my body that had been feeling bound.

People were scattered around the beach with umbrellas and picnic baskets, little kids with plastic buckets running from their parents to the water and back again, topless women and speedo clad men bathing in the sun. We didn't have swimsuits.

It's okay, it's France. We can go with just underwear, Gaal said.

I was hesitant.

Come on, Gaal said laughing. We'll go over there away from all the people.

We walked to an empty part of the beach and spread our towels out on the hot sand. Gaal took off her shorts and top and coaxed me to do the same, then we ran toward the water and dove in. It was cold and salty and perfect. My body felt easy. I scrubbed my scalp, working the salt through, then flipped and squeezed my hair trying to get some of the knots out. Seawater makes my thick hair extra curly. Gaal jumped in the water and shook her head, spinning around, spraying water in loops and spirals. We swam deeper in and lay our backs against the water, floating with the waves like untethered seaweed. I closed my eyes. The sun was hot on my face, the feeling of body held by salt, free and ethereal. Nothingness. I let my mind quiet.

When I was a child, I swam in the Mediterranean in Ashkelon and Tel Aviv every summer, sand gathering in pockets of my swimsuit and crunching in cucumber sandwiches. When I was little, the waves felt so big. Sometimes they tumbled my small body, shoving salt water up my nose and down my throat. Those moments, feeling too small and powerless, humbled me. The sea doesn't discern, it just keeps moving. You have to sync with its rhythm, not the other way around. My mother said, Just float and let the sea hold you, calm you. Give in to the waves and they will wrap you like a blanket.

Gaal swam at the same beaches growing up. We connected about Israel, which temporarily dissolved the things that annoyed me about her. I was annoyed with her, but I wasn't. It wasn't her. It was me.

It's not you it's me.

It's always me.

That is the truest truth.

Myself, my ghost, my self-imposed binding. When you're not free inside, outside is harder to take. In that moment, floating in the sea, nine years old, twenty-three years old, all the same moment, insides matching outside.

Gaal pulled me toward her. She wrapped her legs around my waist and kissed me, floating, weightless. Still free. We swam around, splashed each other, and kissed again until our bodies were exhausted and we had to lie down on the sand, drying off in the hot French sun, the faint sounds of laughing babies echoing down the beach. When we were hot and dry again, we got dressed and rode our loaner bikes back into town toward the hostel, blistering air blowing our hair dry. I felt the sun slowly freckling my skin. We passed a café, a used bookstore, then, a tattoo shop. I stopped.

I want a tattoo, I said.

Let's go in, Gaal said.

I thought about the poppies climbing up the side of her body, how she described the image after showing me the picture of Dee's arm. I could have the picture tattooed onto my body for her, my body, unlike hers, still viable. To give her something she wanted but never had. But even though her body was dissolved, even though that tattoo was never marked into her skin, ultimately it was hers to have. Not mine.

Do you have a tarot deck or book? I asked the tattoo artist.

She didn't understand. Gaal translated. The woman kept her eyes on me as Gaal talked in her easy way, her bright blue almost colorless eyes looking back and forth between us. The artist pulled a box out from under her counter and handed it to me. I thanked her. The box was full of cards, scattered and worn, different tarot decks and playing cards all mixed together. I shuffled them around, searching for the three of swords. The pierced heart, one sword down the middle, the other two at opposing symmetrical angles. I held it up remembering the tarot boy in Dublin, the way his voice said, tenderness. The card's edges were bent like it had been touched many times by many hands. I gave it to the artist and put my finger on the image.

Mmm oui, she said, nodding.

I pointed to my forearm and made an outline with my fingers so she'd know how big. As big as the card, but without the edges. Just the image, heart and swords. She motioned for me to follow her to a vinyl chair, lifting my arm onto a small moveable table beside it. Gaal watched from a couch near the picture window. She was quiet, like she knew that in that moment there was no room for words. The tattoo artist sprayed my arm with a cleaner, then wiped vigorously. She set up her ink and guns and looked at me as if to say, ready? I nodded. She nodded. The gun started to buzz.

I watched black ink bleed into my skin as she began to outline the heart. Her touch was light. She let the gun do the work, moving her hand around, smooth like warm butter. Easy. The stinging of puffy red lines starting to swell felt healing. Like acupuncture.

Needles hitting meridians.

Pressure pressing here to reconcile over there.

She switched from black ink to red, for the heart. Then white around the swords, a twinkle for shine, more black for shading. Less than two hours later, she was finished. It was exactly what I wanted.

We returned the bikes to the hostel then went to the pub next door for a beer. I was high on adrenaline. We drank, we ate, we danced, we sang. And that night, I slept hard in a thin, wrinkled bed. When I opened my eyes in the morning, Gaal was awake.

Let's go to Spain, she said.

It sounded wild to keep going, to go to another country, another new place. But it was no more wild than things had already been. We weren't very far from Barcelona, and I was interested.

We've had good luck hitching so far. I think we can do it, she said.

I followed her lead, the relief of having someone else to make decisions. I knew the feeling wasn't sustainable, but I leaned into it.

Be present.

We gathered our things and walked to the road on the edge of town, thumbs out. After thirty minutes, a small Peugeot pulled over. He was going almost all the way to Barcelona. We got in. Gaal sat up front again, her Spanish better than her French. She chatted with the guy in Spanish at first, then they switched to English. He looked at me through the rearview a few times while he drove. I looked at his bald spot. He was middle aged, nice enough with a minor hint of creepy. After an hour, we pulled over into a small town where he said they had the best falafel. Gaal and I looked at each other knowingly. The best falafel is in Israel. But we didn't tell him that.

We sat at a table outside and he bought our sandwiches and two Oranginas, accepting his generosity and thanking him for paying.

Of course. Listen, he said, I have a half empty apartment right on the beach. It's very nice. I'm helping my son and his wife move out of it, just north of Barcelona. I will drop you there and give you the key. You can stay as long as you want.

Gaal and I shoved falafel and pickles into our mouths and didn't say anything.

I won't bother you. It's there if you want it, he said.

I looked at Gaal. She looked at me. I shrugged. She shrugged.

I'll go to the bathroom and you can talk about it, he said.

He left us at the table and I took a big gulp of soda.

What do you think? she said.

It seems weird to me, I said.

Me too. But if we have the key, we can lock him out.

What if he has another key?

It's an adventure, she said. And it's right on the beach. When will we get to stay somewhere like that?

I don't know, I said.

If he tries to come in with us, we can leave. And we can leave if it feels weird.

Okay, I said, pushing myself into having a new experience.

The apartment was in a cluster of buildings on the beach, as promised, and in a suburb that seemed to be in the middle of nowhere. He pulled the car up to the front door and handed us the key.

If I need to come in you'll have to buzz me up, he said. But I won't come. Enjoy it! When you leave, put the key in the outdoor mailbox.

We thanked him again, still wary but taking the chance. He drove off and we pushed the key into the first door. It worked. We got into an elevator, rode up to the tenth floor, found the apartment, and pushed in the second key. That one worked too. There was a small foyer that opened up to a large living room with

French doors to a balcony and view of the sea. We felt joyous. I noticed a box of baby toys, clothes, and a baby carrier in the corner. I pointed it out to Gaal.

Maybe he is just weird but honest, she said.

The baby stuff makes it seem ok, I said.

We sighed in relief and went to the kitchen to find drinks. The fridge was stocked with bottles of beer, which we promptly opened. We sat on the balcony and I took a deep breath, filling my body with clean salt air. I could live like this. Always near the sea.

See, Gaal said. It's fine.

The more beers I drank, the more fine Gaal's fine became. When my body started to numb, I said, L'Chaim, holding my bottle up to hers. Our bottles clinked.

That night we lay in the bed close to the balcony, keeping the doors open to feel the breeze. I couldn't sleep. The beer wore off and I felt irked again, my guts yelling at me through all the alcohol. I watched one of the French doors sway with the breeze, squeaking just enough to remind me of the creepiness of our situation. But eventually my eyes closed and my body relaxed. At midnight, I was startled awake. Gaal woke too. The apartment buzzer was going off. It buzzed again and again. Then it stopped. We looked at each other. We waited. Then we heard footsteps in the hall.

Get your shit, Gaal said. She jumped out of bed and threw on her shoes. I did the same.

What now? I said.

Now we're ready to run.

We listened. The footsteps crept closer.

Let's go, she said.

We walked toward the door. The handle jiggled from the outside.

We'll just run out when he opens the door, she said.

I lifted out of my body. Disassociate.

Keep moving.

Break the thread.

The door opened.

We held our breath, knees bent, ready to run. He stood in front of us.

I tried to buzz but you didn't answer. I'm sorry if I woke you. I need to get some things, he said.

He took a step into the foyer. The keys clinked, still hanging in their keyhole. As he started to pull the keys out, we squirmed past him out the door and sprinted down the hall to the elevator, looking back over our shoulders every few seconds. He wasn't following us. But we flew into the elevator anyway, still panicked, pushing the door close button over and over until the doors closed. I let my breath out halfway. When we got to the main floor, we jumped out of the elevator looking both ways.

I don't think he's coming, Gaal said. She half laughed.

I pushed open the front door and walked quickly past the parking lot toward the beach. The moon was full, like a single hanging bulb in the sky. She called after me to wait for her. When we got to the sand, I threw down my pack and collapsed.

That was crazy, she said. She laughed all the way.

I wanted to yell. But I said nothing. Don't say what you feel. Avoid conflict.

Are you okay? she said.

Nothing.

What's wrong?

She touched my arm. I pulled it away.

It's not my fault, she said.

It's not? I said.

You agreed, she said.

You decided, I said.

You decided too.

She was right. I did, I decided too. I decided without deciding. Indifference is the illusion you think will save you. It never does. That night, we slept on the beach, too tired to figure out the next move. I looked up at the sky trying to find the Milky Way. The moonlight was too bright. I closed my eyes and listened to the waves, waiting for the sun to bring a new day.

Start again.

I had a dream about my grandfather, Gaal said. He has been sick for a while. I have to go back home. I have a bad feeling.

We were sitting on the beach side by side, watching the sky lighten, like a dimmer switch being turned up. I didn't look at her, and I didn't feel her eyes looking at me.

Will you come back with me? She said.

I was running out of money. And I was ready to be alone again, knowing I'd have to go back to America soon. Her impulsive choices were starting to bind me. I wanted to be free. Unwrap, unravel. I took a deep breath with an incoming wave and breathed out with the ebb. All eyes still on the horizon. She waited. She knew without knowing. So did I.

I'm going to Barcelona, I said. I decided in that moment.

The corners of her eyes dropped.

Are you still mad? she said.

I'm sorry, I said.

I didn't say yes or no. I was, and I wasn't. I wanted to and I didn't.

We continued looking at the sea in silence. I saw a whale arc through the water. I wondered if she saw it too. Eventually the sun heated our bodies enough to push us into making a move. I got up and propped my pack onto my back, then reached out my hand to help her up. We walked toward the buildings looking for someone who could give us directions to the train. A middle-aged woman pulling groceries out of her car pointed out the way. The station was just a few blocks away, a one-room building with printed schedules stacked neatly in plastic containers along the wall. We were right on time.

A train going north, a train going south. Hers came first.

You can still change your mind, Gaal said, knowing I wouldn't.

I hugged her. She kissed me. I kissed back. Then she was gone.

27.

When you're in precarious situations, just be quiet and follow along. That way you don't have to decide. I knew this wasn't a good motto to live by, but it was the one I chose, or fell into, or followed along. Leader, follower, follower, leader. Chicken or egg. The driver was an older guy from a different high school, a friend of her sister. He played music with her boyfriend, bought us beer, and drove us around sometimes.

You guys owe me a buck and a quarter for your forties, he said from the driver's seat.

Her boyfriend was in the passenger seat and we sat in back. We gave him a handful of loose coins and reached into a paper bag on the floor of the back seat, keeping the bottles low, leaning down and forward to drink. When someone spotted a cop car, she and I looked at each other, yelled FIVE-O! and hugged our bottles between our knees, laughing. He drove fast, east toward the lake. Sometimes he drove so fast I had to squeeze my eyes shut and remind myself how much I didn't care if I died.

Close your eyes and the danger disappears.

I read Zen and the Art of Motorcycle Maintenance. I read Be Here Now. I heard Alan Watts talk about how big the universe was and how tiny and inconsequential we were. I understood that I was not in control of any of it.

Let go, be free.

We made it to the lake without getting pulled over, crashing, or spilling any beer and sat on the shore looking out at the horizon. Lake Michigan is like the ocean. You can't see the other side. I had drunk a third of my forty in the car and was drunk. Everyone called me a lightweight. She took my forty and said, I can drink the whole thing. We all cheered her on. I hugged her and laughed.

I have to pee, come with me, she said.

We walked to a tree far enough away so that they couldn't see us. She squatted.

Cover me, she said.

I turned my back to her and spread my short arms wide. She laughed at my attempt and I laughed at her laughing. When we got back to the group, the driver lit a joint and passed it around. We sat on the beach side by side watching boats float in the water far off in the distance, running our hands through the dirty city sand, the smell of dead fish and saltwater.

I'm gonna puke, I said. The beer, the joint, the dead salty fish.

I'll hold your hair, she said.

I jumped up and ran to the parking lot and she followed. She grabbed my hair just as I leaned over between two cars, a stream of fizzy beer released.

I'm okay, I said, standing back up and wiping my mouth on the edge of my sleeve.

You're okay, she said.

We high-fived and then she put her arm around me. It's amazing how much better you can feel after a good puke. When we got back to the shore, her boyfriend was sitting back against a tree. She straddled his lap and immediately started making out with him. The driver was sitting right where we had left him, smoking another joint and looking out at the water, unaffected. He passed me the joint without looking at me. I ignored her, pretending to be happy sitting with this random guy on the smelly Chicago beach smoking a joint in silence.

28.

The first train south cruised along the coast toward Figueres. My guidebook said the town was famous for the Salvador Dali Museum. I put my headphones on, Jane's Addiction's Three Days playing in the middle of the song:

We chose no kin but adopted strangers / The family weakens by the length we travel.

The coastline rushed by through smudgy, half open windows and smelled of perfect turquoise blue. At each stop I watched teenagers get on and off the train, laughing and pushing each other and swinging around the vertical holding poles wearing nothing but swimsuits and short shorts. I watched them, invisible in my plastic chair inside a bubble of sound. Momentarily free. I hadn't been alone, all alone, for a long time. There was nowhere I needed to be and no one I planned to meet. I let my bubble wrap itself around me like a protective hand knit sweater. When the train stopped in the center of town, I got off. The streets were quiet, the air sea-salty and warm. I thought about her voice, but I didn't feel her there.

The guidebook pointed me to a small, cheap hotel down a narrow street. I rented a room just big enough for a bed with a shared hallway bathroom. Simple and sufficient. It was exactly what I needed. I dropped my bag in the corner of the room and went down to the lobby for a map, ready to spend the entire day alone staring at Dali paintings. Two young Japanese tourists, a guy and a girl, were trying to communicate with the receptionist. My Spanish wasn't good, but it was better than theirs. I asked if they spoke English.

A little, the girl said.

She told me they were trying to rent a room for three nights. I explained they needed to show their passports and told the person at the desk, tres noches. He smiled and nodded. They offered to buy me a beer as a thank you. My money was running low and though I wanted to be alone, I also really wanted a beer.

We found a small café a few doors down from the hotel and sat at a table shaded by a multi-colored umbrella. A perfect breeze moved around us under the canopy. My body felt light. Being aware of my things and my physicality, my heavy pack and the weight of romance, was exhausting. I opened my palms wide, slid my shoulders down my back, and let all of it fall.

The relief of space.

The relief of Spain.

I ordered three cervezas. We raised our bottles and smiled at each other. I took a huge gulp of beer, the bubbles fizzing and stinging the inside of my chest and down, into my stomach. I love the heat of the first sip of booze. They asked if I was traveling alone.

Sort of, I said.

I waved my hands in the air, wiggling my fingers, looking up and around.

You're never alone. Even though you're always alone, the guy said.

Always both, the girl laughed.

Always both, I said.

We finished our beers and I thanked them. They thanked me back, again, and I got up to leave.

Go toward adventure and be free, the girl said.

I smiled and said, you too.

They had each other and I was happy to just have myself.

Salvador Dali lived in Figueres and was buried under the museum, a grand and colorful building full of windows and light and magic. His paintings always calmed me, the realism inside of the absurd; clean lines of an otherwise chaotic idea. Magic where there shouldn't be any, or magic where you need it most. I walked around the museum for hours. I sat in front of a three-story painting. I watched pictures move without moving, trick of the eye, trick of the mind. There are no still images. Everything breathes, you just have to look closely, be still to make space for breath that is not your own. I watched and found my breath inside of and in sync with the colors, his thin mustached face, skinny-legged animals and melting clocks, the world without edges, soft and stealthy and round. All one thing. I wanted to stay in Spain, but the circle was closing. The beginning and the end starting to touch. I knew I had to go back, wherever back even was.

That night, I sank my body into the small bed in the small room and dreamed about her face in my face close up, her eyes shining behind distorted images of Dali's tigers and misshapen pomegranates reflected in her glasses. Her image separating into moving bubbles like Galatea of the Spheres and the sound of her laugh so loud it woke me with a start. I sat up, forgetting where I was. A small moonbeam coming in through a high window gave me enough light to see, to remember. I looked at my hands. We always look at our hands in the dark to measure the distance light allows. I looked around the room. Shadows moved up the walls, cast from trees outside, pushed by the wind. I felt her again, the way dreams connect the veils. I felt her and I wanted to feel her more, to see her face close up like in the dream, her breath, small and thin, blanketing me. I wanted to kiss her one last time. My face fell into my hands and I let myself sob. I let my body shake and spasm until it was exhausted.

And then, my guts said, you're too far away. Go home.

I took a deep breath, then many more deep breaths to lull my mind back to sleep. Breathe in, hold it hold it hold it, breathe out slow. Again. Again. The switch in my mind finally clicked, this time without dreams. She let me rest.

When I woke, the sun was barely up but I was ready. I got dressed and took the first train to the airport.

PART 2

29.

The plane landed in New York and I was alone. Again. I took a bus to Virginia. Not to her father's house, but to a new unfamiliarity in a now familiar place. Different reasons, old new place. New old place. Unsteady heartbeat. Pumping pumping.

I went to Virginia for one reason and also for another. I'd heard about a meditation center in the Shenandoah Valley, one I thought I'd never visit. I never thought I'd visit Virginia in the first place, and certainly not in the second place. The things we think won't happen find their way around if they want to. No way to resist certainty. I had done a ten-day silent meditation course in Washington the previous year. It was one of the hardest voluntary experiences I had been through, and also, it brought me into the lightest I had ever felt. This certainty I was certain I wanted to experience again. This one was easy to lean into.

The bus ride from New York to Virginia was long and dirty. I put my headphones on, tightening the metal headband all the way, knowing my head would bob side to side as I fell in and out of sleep. And to keep people away, which I always thought would work but rarely did. As night arrived and the bus lights dimmed, the guy behind me whisper-yelled through the crack between our seats, his breath hot on my neck and the sound waves of his voice snaking and tangling in my hair.

Hey girl wanna see something? Hey back here behind you, he said.

I closed my eyes tight and rolled my fingers along the jagged knob that turned up the volume. Ignoring people is a form of self-care. He might have kept talking to me, but I let the music take up all the sound space. I imagined a protective bubble around my body, then around my whole seat, and sank into the comfort of familiar song lyrics. The music lulled me into a music video sleep, but I woke just as the bus pulled into the Harrisonburg station. As soon as I heard that gas release bus stopping sound, I jumped out of my seat and ran to the front before anyone else could get up, creating as much distance between my body and hot breath guy as possible. I found a payphone with a thick phone book attached by a chain just outside the station and called the meditation center. The next ten-day course wasn't starting for two days, but they said I could help clean and prepare food until then. Jo, a new volunteer, would pick me up in twenty minutes.

Jo arrived in a rusty blue Honda Civic, the kind with only two doors so you have to push the front seat forward to get into the back. I immediately knew who she was. She looked at me through her open window and said my name, not as a question, but a statement.

Throw your bag in the back, it's open, she said.

I got into the passenger seat and we shook hands. Her eyes were the color of milk chocolate if chocolate were made of seawater, perfect round marbles that didn't look away first. She didn't ask where I'd been or where I was going or why, which made me like her more than I liked her eyes and her open face. We didn't talk, but she smiled for most of the twenty minute drive, singing along to the slow Cure Disintegration tape in her tape deck. I didn't tell her how much I loved that album, but I sang along also smiling, feeling the wind on my face through the rolled down windows. I breathed deep, pulling the newly familiar Virginia air hard into my body.

When I was a kid, my dad taught me that if you blink fast looking at a moving fan, you can see all of its blades, singular, and that's how you know how many blades it has. As I watched oaks and poplars pass by along the road, I blinked my eyes, open close open close, separating the moving images into stills. I told myself to remember this moment, these photographs in my eyes and the feeling of smiling without effort.

Jo pulled the car into a gravel lot.

Grab your bag and follow me, she said.

We walked down a wooded path and came to the main center. There was a lobby with pamphlets, a dining hall to the left, and a kitchen behind the dining hall. To the right was an adjacent door that led through a dark hallway into the women's quarters. Jo told me to pick an empty bed, get settled, then come back to the kitchen. I dropped my bag on a bed at the farthest corner near a window and sat. Outside was a field with a track where we would be allowed to walk and stretch our legs during the meditation course. Beyond the field, more woods. I focused my eyes as far as they could see. At the edge of the field where the woods began, I saw something moving. I squinted. I made circles with my hands around my eyes like binoculars. I focused harder. The image moved closer, its eyes shiny black. As it approached, I saw the small white spots along its torso. It jumped, as if for joy, then was followed by another. Two fawns. Meditation deer. I wanted to hug them, to lay in the grass with them and feel their noses touching my face. My heart felt big. I was exactly where I was supposed to be.

There were two other people in the kitchen, a young man and a young woman. They introduced themselves as Jessie and Jackie. They were a couple. I was endeared by their names and the seemingly tight but relaxed thread between them. Jo was there too. We all smiled at each other and Jo put me to work on some dishes while she dried and put them away. Jessie and Jackie chopped vegetables, preparing dinner for the four of us. They had been at the center for two months, long-term volunteers.

The practice has taught us how to get through storms, Jessie said.

Storms? I said.

Fights. Blowouts. Anger, he said.

I can't imagine being with someone who doesn't have a practice, Jackie said.

We totally get each other now that we meditate together, Jessie said.

They looked at each other with twinkly eyes the way you do when you're so in love it makes the people around you feel sick and also, jealous. I nodded. I wanted that, someone to meditate with, someone who knew how to weather their own storms or weather storms together.

Accountability.

Self-reflection.

Connection.

And also, I believed them, but I didn't believe in them. I thought they'd probably split up after they finally left the center, which I did not say out loud. They were young and idealistic. It was beautiful and hopeful and sad to watch them, that feeling of knowing someone's future without knowing how you know. But definitely knowing.

An old friend once told me about how she observed the different ways we can be psychic according to our elemental astrology charts. She said, when you have a lot of fire, you have the kind of psychic ability to know something is going to happen without evidence or the logic to prove it. You just know in a deeply certain way. And then it happens.

Jo was looking at me, watching for my reaction. She didn't roll her eyes, but her smile told me she knew what I was thinking. I smiled the same way back at her.

After dinner, I walked past the field toward the woods watching the sunset turn the sky deep purple and neon pink-orange, bats circling overhead. I was grateful for rural air and to be back on a familiar continent, safe and still for at least the next twelve days. I walked slow, peeking between tree branches looking for the fawns. I heard rustling but the sound was too small for deer.

Squirrels or chipmunks or birds or maybe more bats. I hoped anyway. I called to the fawns in my mind, thinking about their black opal eyes and their fuzzy spotted bodies moving around me. Sometimes you can think your way into circumstance. But the fawns didn't arrive. I told the woods I would be back and asked if they might come out again, to refill the space in my chest.

You can't get attached to anything or anyone at a meditation center. There are rules, spoken and unspoken. When the ten days of silence begins, they tell you not to make eye contact with your fellow meditators, not to read or write or exercise heavily or talk to anyone unless it's an absolute emergency. The idea isn't one of deprivation or to follow a leader, rather to have an experience like that of a monk, to be able to go deep into yourself and the practice without any distractions. I was already distracted.

Jo asked me to help her get the meditation room ready for the participants. She made piles of cushions and set up the teacher's area at the front of the room while I swept the corners and wiped cobwebs. I asked how long she was staying at the center.

I'm heading west after this course, she said.

Me too, I said.

She smiled.

Could you give me a ride? I said.

Of course. Where are you going?

I don't know.

I'm going to New Mexico, she said.

Me too, I said again.

She smiled and touched my shoulder, looking at my eyes too long. She never looked away first. When I finally looked down, she pulled her hand back and said, I'm going to town to take care of some personal matters. I'll be back tomorrow morning to greet the participants as they arrive. Check in with Jessie and Jackie if you need anything else.

I nodded and she left, latching the door so quietly I thought she might've walked through the wall instead of using the door. I pushed two big cushions together and lay on my back. The ceiling was a perfectly symmetrical graph of thin overlapping wood planks with a whirring fan hanging down exactly in the middle. I blinked quickly.

Five blades.

The course hadn't started yet, but I couldn't wait for New Mexico. I knew the next ten days would be the longest of my life.

30.

The last time, the first time I was in Virginia, I met her Buddhist mom. Her eyes the same maritime blue eyes, the rest of her face too familiar for never even having seen a picture.

Are you angry? She asked me. Because I am, she said. She was smiling.

I was confused. I didn't answer, feeling more coming.

I'm not angry that she died. I'm angry that she chose to die. That she decided to leave us, her mom said.

I half smiled, less of a smile than her smile, an acknowledgment of her pain, her non-anger anger. Without being a parent, I understood her loss to be one I could not grasp. I was, in the midst of enduring loss myself, somewhat dissociated.

I'd like for you to light a stick of incense as we say the death prayer, she said.

I nodded. She was still smiling. She touched my arm with a cold, clammy hand, and walked toward the altar. I followed her. She rang a bell and people gathered. Her sister and dad joined her mom, each of them lighting a few candles, then her mom invited people to come up and light incense as she began to chant. One by one we walked up. Her dad handed out sticks to be lit off one of the candles, then we circled back. The house filled with smoke. I tried not to cough. My eyes stung. I focused on the smoke coming off of one stick as it rose, curly then straight then wide then blended with the rest. The smoke seemed to hear the chanting, synchronizing like a wistful dance. Emotion is so affected by woven senses. Crying and numb together.

I wasn't angry. I used to think everyone thought about suicide, constructed a plan to lean into when life was too much. A way out, a relief. That was my coping technique. There were times I got close enough to touch it, gathering pills or blades. The physicality of seeing and tracing, knowing I could push the eject button anytime, was enough of an edge to bump into. Lingering thoughts meant to soothe. Actualizing those plans are where the boundary changes. What is enough for one person is peanuts for another. I wasn't surprised she actualized. She tried to stay in her body. She tried to turn inside out, energize her light, push and lean into the goodness. But all she got was peanuts.

We get to choose.

She chose.

And who am I to judge that choice?

31.

The first day is the longest. The second day is the hardest. On the third day, someone always leaves, the feeling of imprisonment wrapping tight around thoughts, body, spirit. The mind grows louder than it has ever been. It drudges up shame, insecurity, mistakes, and pulses on physical pain. It's true, we make our own prisons. I wanted to leave, and I knew I wouldn't.

Those first days, my insides moved like wild storm clouds preparing for a tornado. Things grew dark and the container of my body felt too small, unable to hold its contents. We were instructed to notice the sensation of breath around our nostrils, cold hot odors movement. The mind can't really multitask. When you focus on one thing, there's little room for much else. The challenge is the switch, jumping around from one thing to the next. I kept coming back. I tried. By the third day, the instruction was to move from the nostrils to the entire body. Notice the scalp, the face, the shoulders, all the way down then all the way back up. Up and down, down and up. I reached hard and deep past the garbage into moments of body vibration that suddenly felt good. The moments came and went. They told us not to get attached to the good feelings just like not to attach to the hard ones.

Don't attach to any of it.

I attached.

Everyone attaches.

Mediation is like drugs but wholesome. When I couldn't connect, when my mind wouldn't let me go and my body ached, I thought about sex and burritos and chocolate cake and the smell of rain and the lyrics to songs I loved. I found books in my mind and movies of my life, decent memories that often turned sour without my consent. Then, when I'd had enough, reset back into the practice. Watch the breath, scan the body, quiet the mind. When they did come, the euphoria was extraordinary. My body disappeared. I became as free as I imagined I would ever be, what death was probably like, blended back into the atmosphere. In those moments, I didn't think about her. I didn't think about anything.

We sat first thing in the morning, then tea and food and more sitting. Lunch, walking, searching for fawns, more sitting, more food, more sitting. By the fifth day, I was used to the pattern and the struggle eased. I settled in. My body released tension and my mind stopped counting days. I sat and the freedom arrived more and more quickly.

And then, the fawns returned. A reward for my hard work.

On day six, I woke with the sun and the morning bell that signaled the first sit of the day. Through the window beside the bed, they were much closer than before. I could see the hairs on their necks blowing as the wind picked up, their ears twitching around bird songs, and their tongues tasting the grass. So close, too close, not close enough. I slid my shoes on and walked outside, slow, methodical, breathing quietly and talking to the fawns in my mind, telling them they could trust me. My eyes met the eyes of one of the fawns. She looked back at me.

Neither of us looking away first.

Her eyes black, then sea blue.

Animals are always meditating.

Some people think when you leave your body, you are born into another. I saw her in the fawn. I heard her voice through those black blue black eyes.

She said, I never left and I never will.

I see you, I said.

We are always everywhere.

Jo hadn't been around much for the first half of the course, but she joined the evening sit on day six, setting her cushion up next to mine. She came in late. My eyes were closed but I felt her. I tried to stay focused on my breath, sensation in my body, feet legs torso hands arms face head, then back down again. But the edge of her buzz pressed against the edge of mine. If you face your palms toward each other close enough to almost touch without touching, you can feel the edge. It's hot and tingly. We don't end at the surface of our skin. In the way that we are not our bodies, but inside, around, habituating them. Our vitality extends further, like a personal ozone layer.

When the bell rang, I opened my eyes and looked down at her hands resting in her lap. I knew I wasn't supposed to look at her, and I knew she wouldn't look at me. But she flipped the hand closest to me and made the smallest gesture of a wave. I waved back and she put her thumb and forefinger together in an okay sign. She got up to go to dinner and I followed. I stood behind her in line and sat next to her at the dining table. Meals were quiet except for the clank of silverware and people taking deep breaths. We were encouraged to eat slowly, mindfully, which prompted a lot of people to sigh as they ate. Sighing seems dramatic but it's really a way to just oxygenate your body and relax. No one looked up. We sat on a long bench at a long table. I slid my legs a little wider, careful to tap my knee against hers. She didn't flinch and she didn't scoot it away. It felt electric. I didn't know if it was because of the meditation, the heightened awareness of sensation, or chemistry between us. I dissolved my body by being embodied. My body felt better because I gave it more space. I wanted to be free and also, I wanted to feel all the sensations.

She got up first.

She always got up first. But she never looked away first.

That night, I dreamed I woke in the bed I was sleeping in at the center. I floated up and walked through the window toward the fawn I had spoken to, my body made of the same material as the wall as though all of it were water, easy to move around. I wrapped my arms around her furry neck and, as I hugged her, she became my ghost. Her hands moved up and down my back and rested between my legs. I pulled away to look at her and she was Jo. Her eyes, Jo's eyes, fawn eyes. She leaned in to kiss me and I kissed back, her lips warm and full. Her mouth tasted like whiskey and strawberries and the way that first sip of booze goes down, tingling the chest in warmth. We breathed together, her exhale pulled into my inhale, her inhale pressed into my exhale. The intimacy of sharing breath with someone, feeling its heat so close, is what makes kissing familiar. Connecting faces, eyes too close they blur. The kiss seemed to last for hours. During the next morning's sit, I wondered if she'd had the same dream.

When I was in high school, I dreamed about a girl I barely knew in my history class. We were running in a field, looking at each other and laughing as though we were best friends. The next day in class, she approached me, telling me she had dreamed about me the night before. As she described her dream, she described mine. I told her I had the same dream. She didn't believe me, thinking I was mocking her, and walked away in anger. Connecting through the layers of thin webbing seems unlikely, mostly because we don't believe in it. But there is no such thing as coincidence. We are not so separate. Psychic fire. It's possible to tangle our wires when we let go, like we do in sleep. In fact, it's likely. We just don't acknowledge it because we've been taught that anything we can't physically prove isn't real.

I wanted to tell Jo about the dream. I wanted to kiss her and to kiss my ghost and to kiss the fawn and be wrapped in the connective tissue of sleep and love. But I didn't. There are so many moments of almost that fall away because we are afraid.

32.

The winter after we moved in together, we went snow hiking in the mountains outside of town. Greg lived in the communal house where I had lived, where she lived after me. He was an outdoorsy adventure dude, and offered to take us along with one of his other roommates on a cold, sunny Saturday. We bundled ourselves in layers of clothes and headed out in Greg's pickup. The mountain was sharp and magical. We walked up a steep trail and as we entered the woods, the snow was untouched, fresh like soft serve ice cream. It sparkled in the sun and I wanted to lay in it, roll my body around in its whipped creaminess. The air felt clean in my lungs. I was happy.

Greg walked ahead, his roommate behind, then the two of us. We walked fast, feeling the sun warming our bodies from the outside and our momentum warming us inside. I took off my coat and Greg stripped down to a T-shirt, the freedom of single layers in the middle of winter. Our steps were steady and our breathing heavy. We hiked up higher, then straight ahead, then higher again until we were at the uppermost trail. She loved being away from the city. Her face softened and her body eased. She was the most calm and centered outside, when there were more trees than people around.

An hour in, clouds arrived and the snow began to fall. Greg said they were just flurries and would pass quickly. We all marveled at the twinkly beauty. I scooped chunks of creamy snow into my mouth. Snowballs were thrown. Snow angels were made. The flurries, however, quickly turned into heavier flakes and the trail began to disappear. Greg assured us he knew the way through. But as the snow thickened under our feet, he admitted he'd lost the trail. Soon we found ourselves on a steep edge where we had to dig our poles into the snow with each step so we wouldn't tumble down the mountain. Another hour passed. Night approached. The sun reflecting snow went from bright white to gray. I thought about that movie where a plane crashes in the snowy mountains and the people have to eat each other to survive, some freezing to death in the nighttime snow. I could feel Greg's distress, though he kept reassuring us we'd make it out before the sky was fully dark, my own fear and the roommate's looming. Hers though, never came.

I never felt her fear, even when she was angry. Sometimes anger is just about the need for love. Most fear is ultimately wrapped in death. Without the fear of death, fear is nearly dissolved. I tried to attach to her unattached love. She didn't say it, but I knew part of her didn't care if we made it out. I wanted to not care either. I wanted to remember that leaving the body behind is not an end, but a freedom to something new. I wanted to relax into the disorder, trust the universe, submit to the grandness that was out of my hands one way or another.

We walked. The snow persevered. My feet got cold and numb, then tingly, but I didn't complain. Greg kept us moving hard and fast. Stay focused, don't think about the future, feel each step. Be here now. The only thing to do is to keep going. Then, just as the light of day was about to fully disappear, we reached the trailhead. He pointed, yelled, and smiled big. We all clapped and ran toward the truck, sighing. He passed out the beers he had stashed under the seats. I chugged mine quickly and he drove us back to town. I told him I'd never go hiking with him again and everyone laughed. He said that's what adventure is all about. She nodded in agreement. I looked at her with wide eyes and she shrugged her shoulders, sipping her beer.

None of it really matters, she said. All or nothing.

33.

That last sit on the tenth day was a relief. As I settled in one last time, I felt the weight of the entire room lift. A throat was cleared. Someone coughed. Then a fart and several people started laughing. I squeezed my eyes shut trying to hold my laugh in, but it only made me laugh harder. The room erupted. Crying and laughing are the same kind of release. Emotions moving up and out with sound, tears, and letting go. The bell rang and the teacher requested we stack our cushions as we left the room. After the noontime meditation, the silence was broken. We were encouraged to talk and make eye contact with the other participants, to share experiences and make plans to form meditation groups with people who lived in our towns and cities. To re-enter being social people in society. It was a strange feeling, sitting everyday with all these people I'd never met, never seeing them or being seen, never hearing their voices or learning about their lives, even though we felt each other. Bodies are not the only way to bond. But also, hearing voices, looking at eyes, seeing and being seen makes faces become alive and more beautiful.

Once outside, I felt a hand on my shoulder. I turned to see Jo.

Have you seen the fawns? she said.

Jo's eyes, her eyes, deer eyes.

My eyes in the reflection.

I nodded.

Let's go find them, she said.

We walked through the field to the edge of the woods. Jo pushed some branches back to reveal a narrow deer trail. I followed her in. We walked slow and discreet without talking. It was late summer, the sounds of crickets and geese passing through the sky, small bird songs and crows in the distance. A strong breeze pressed through my body. I felt like a kid creeping around looking for an adventure. We arrived at a meadow on the other side of the woods and came upon a huge old oak, like the one in Ireland. I looked for her up in the highest curling branch. I was in Virginia after all, the last place she lived inside her body. I took a deep breath and smelled the smoke.

You can leave me here, she said.

She was looking down at me, blowing smoke rings, one through another.

Seriously, she said. But first come up here.

I climbed up and she opened her arms wide. She was leaning back against the branch, her legs hanging over either side. I folded forward, hugging thick bark. It smelled like smoke and vanilla. I kissed the branch, her lips, scratchy tree skin. She was there and, she wasn't.

I love this tree, Jo said. She climbed up to meet me.

We dangled our legs over the branch's edge sitting side by side, looking out into the meadow. She put her hand next to mine. Our pinkies touched. I didn't look at her but I didn't move my hand. And then the fawns arrived, this time with their mother. They didn't seem to see us. We held our breath as we watched them from above, eating and flipping their ears and tails. The doe looked up at me. Recognition in her eyes. Her face was the most familiar one I had ever seen.

34.

I threw my bag into the trunk of Jo's Honda and waved goodbye to the meditation center. Jo turned up the volume on the stereo. The Cure tape was still playing. I hadn't heard music in ten days. It felt loud and also relieving, like a new episode was arriving as the last one fell away. I wanted to leave her in Virginia, to shed the past and move forward, unattached.

I had this dream, Jo said.

We hadn't talked for the entire duration of side A and side B of the tape. After being silent for over a week, I didn't feel there was much that needed saying. I acclimated to silence, to the thoughts in my head passing without anyone else experiencing them, and that became okay. Most of what happens in my head doesn't need to be shared. But I turned down the music, looking at Jo as she looked at the road.

You were there, she said. And there was a girl I didn't know. She hugged me and then pushed me into you.

Jo didn't look at me. She didn't blush and her voice didn't waver.

Sometimes my dreams feel more real than my waking, I said.

I feel that, she laughed.

She turned to me for a second, the way you do when you're driving, smiling like she knew something about me that I hadn't told her. I knew the girl she described in her dream. She knew the girl too. Dreams are not separate, but rather the other side or another side of the stories we live, moving slides sewn together, a place to make sense of things that are otherwise senseless.

We arrived in Nashville as the sun was setting. Jo had an old friend there with a pull-out couch bed she offered to us for the night. Her friend greeted us with hot plates of spaghetti and beer. I ate slow, breathing and sighing, trying to stay mindful. It was already difficult. It takes so much work to get there, and none to leave. Like baking bread. You mix and knead and wait for it to rise and shape it and wait for it to rise again and to bake and to cool, hours and hours, sometimes more than one day, and it can be eaten in seconds. Gone.

We brushed our teeth and wrapped ourselves in the comforter on the squeaky pull out bed, lying side by side, looking at each other. She took my hand. I tangled my fingers with hers and she leaned her face into my face. We kissed for a long time. Her mouth felt familiar and comforting like in my dream, a place to stay steady for a while. We kissed until I fell asleep, unaware of when the kissing ended and sleep began.

When I woke in the morning, I was alone in the bed. I heard them talking in the kitchen.

Does she know? the friend said.

She's in Virginia and I'm not going back, Jo said.

I got out of bed and walked toward the kitchen, trying to be loud so they'd hear me coming.

Good morning, I said.

Jo handed me a cup of tea.

We should get going, she said.

I nodded and thanked the friend. She smiled in a kind way and then looked at Jo, still smiling but a little bit sideways. I pretended not to notice.

Are you okay? I asked Jo when we were back on the road.

That day I left the center to take care of personal stuff, she said.

I nodded, remembering.

I've been going through a breakup, she said. I went to the center to get clear.

Sorry, I said.

She shrugged.

Nothing stays the same forever, she said.

We both left someone in Virginia, I said.

She smiled. I knew she knew without me having to tell her.

I'm not going back. Only forward, she said.

Start again, I said.

That's the whole thing, she said. That's all of it.

Part of the guidance in the meditation course was to keep starting again. Keep coming back. Each time you lose focus, every time you fall off, start over. Start again, the teacher's voice would say at the beginning of each sit, in the middle, toward the end.

Start again.

Starting again.

We started again.

35.

The lines of ourselves are drawn in pencil, thin and erasable. Not like comic strips with thick black borders that hold in all the shape and color. When we sleep, our lines get thinner, dreams diluting what we think is our reality. Even in reality, the lines bleed when they get wet from tears sweat heat love.

Dreaming and waking, embodied and ethereal, all one thing.

When I was in Virginia, in her room, in her closet, around the ashes of her body and the incense of her family, I saw the open phone book she left on a desk in the corner, her passport, her ID, and her social security card lined neatly in a row beneath it. The first heading read, loss of a loved one, and below that were therapists and groups and centers focused on dealing with death.

She knew she was loved.

She was a loved one and we had loss.

Her parents had no doubt seen it but it looked untouched, almost unnoticed. A thing too heavy to acknowledge. I ran my fingers around the words, the pages thin and flimsy as they are in phonebooks, versatile as toilet paper when needed. I leaned my nose in to smell the ink and dust, searching for the scent of bitter herbs and body odor. I pressed the tip of my tongue into the words then lay my cheek against its coolness. I wanted to take the book with me, knowing they would probably leave it there forever intact, unscathed.

36.

We drove through Tennessee, Arkansas, and Oklahoma, sleeping in cheap motels or driving through the night in shifts. The nights we had a bed I fell into deep, hard sleeps, exhausted from the travel. We listened to my Jane's Addiction tapes, more Cure, some mixes and country radio when it came in, for fun. Sometimes we sat in silence, the sound of the road and wind filling in the space. She didn't ask about my life, I didn't ask about hers. We had a silent understanding of privacy and knowing our lanes were only crossed temporarily, thin webbing traversed for the purpose of movement, to get somewhere else. But we had moments of offering.

The girl in the dream, Jo said as we drove through the upper part of Texas. You loved her.

I nodded.

She was there at the oak, and in your dream, I said.

I know, she said.

You saw her on the tree?

I saw you see her. In my dream, she told me to help you let her go.

I didn't mean to, but I started crying. They said things like this could happen after sitting in silence for ten days, big emotions, physical rashes, bursts of anger and headaches. Stuckness gets unlatched and starts to move around the body. Jo kept her eyes on the road ahead and, without looking, pulled a handkerchief from her back pocket and handed it to me. I wrapped it around my face, folding forward, my head in my hands resting on my legs. She put a hand on my back. The weight of her hand held a heat full of uncomplicated love. I cried harder. I cried through Texas until we got to the New Mexico border and when we arrived, I was ready to leave her for good, all the way back in Virginia.

We drove into the hills outside of Santa Fe where Jo had lived a few years back. Her friends started an outdoor gay circus there, performing on makeshift trapezes draped from trees to the soundtrack of musicians playing old trumpets and drums made of pots and buckets and hand carved flutes. There were juggling clowns, group song interludes, and hula hooping comedy sketches. Her friends offered a small adobe cabin for us to stay in. They fed us tempeh tacos with homemade sauerkraut and hot sauce so hot it made me sweat as soon as I swallowed. I loved it. New Mexico was arid and sizzling and dried out all of my weeping. The meditation course pressed itself behind me, pushed up against my back, and moved me forward into the desert, up and out. Extracted.

Start again.

Keep moving.

Or maybe, be still and let the movement happen around you.

She told me to leave her behind and I wanted to. I desperately wanted to.

I stayed with Jo in New Mexico for a week, helping her set up tents for the circus. I watched rehearsals, danced with new friends to the band as they played music around bonfires every night, and drank local tequila with fresh lime and chunky salt. Jo and I slept on a small futon on the ground, watching tiny lizards scamper across the concrete floor in awe. We kissed at night when the lights went out, but we never talked about it and we never moved past kissing. Kissing was our way of connecting without words. Sharing breath without the vibration of text sound. We meditated in the mornings, but I knew we would never have storms like Jessie and Jackie. You can't have storms without complicated love. Neither of us opened those gates. We weren't ready, or we just weren't the ones for each other.

The night before the opening night, a final dress rehearsal was performed for everyone involved in creating the circus. Sturdy trapeze ropes were hung from two thick branches of an oak tree that sat behind the stage. Spotlights were set up using generators. And the band gathered in a corner, bucket drums and an electric guitar with a portable amp just for the trapeze acts. I had seen them intermittently, but not all the way through with costumes, lights, and music.

Jo and I sat together in the front row. The sun sank and the trapeze began. Two people side by side, twins in matching striped bodysuits and a light shining between them. The electric guitar started, one note at a time on reverb, vibrating around the ropes around their limbs. Their bodies moved in arcs of breath, backward inhale forward exhale. They seemed to move with my own breath. With everyone's breath, sighing. All the sharp edges and angles of physical lines rounded out like branches of the oak tree they hung from.

All the oak trees in all the places, holding all the secrets.

Oak trees can live to be three hundred years old. They're like great ancestors, growing the past into the present.

The trapeze artists were animals in an animal dance, seeing only the other, curling upside-down, wrapping pieces of themselves around rope, suspending, holding and swinging each other, slow, still, quick, tangled. At times they were so synced, each a mirage of the other reflected against their physicality like a wiped clean mirror. Then, moments of holding each other so tight, no beginning or end to their body structures. The love between them was brutal in a way that it couldn't have been just a performance. They were lovers with unimaginable trust.

The spotlight shown in their faces. I could see the charge between their eyes so clear. They were all of it. The whole of a relationship, twined together, held up, reflected, touching without touching, and then so snarled they became the other or disappeared completely. Both and. I wanted to be them. And also, I was repulsed. The feeling of wanting something so intimate it makes you sick. Or knowing if I had it, I'd never be able to keep it alive.

A break in the chain breaks the whole chain.

Tenderness is the most delicate thing.

I felt Jo's eyes on my cheek. I didn't look at her because I didn't want to explain even though I knew I didn't have to. She held my hand and squeezed it. Not tender but grounded. I didn't have any more tears. The desert had dried me out and though all the feelings swirled in my chest, for the first time I saw us from a distance. What I thought was one thing, or a collage of things smashed together into one messy pile, was something else. Many other things threaded together tight in some places and nearly severed in others. Unmendable. Because that's how it comes together when you don't know how to animal dance with someone. I saw the sad blue of her seawater eyes in my eyes and the distance we were never able to span, even when we were touching.

I squeezed Jo's hand back and smiled, then let go and walked back to the cabin for a glass of salty rimmed tequila. I walked to the edge of the property. The air smelled smokey and cool and made me feel free. I was thinking about the west coast. Home. Time to slow down, the end of summer chaos starting to wane. Work, community, my own bed, stillness called in a new way. My heart had changed. I breathed and cried and meditated all the crap out of my body and it was time to arrive in my growth. Rosh Hashanah, the Jewish new year, happens in the beginning of fall with the new moon of September. The culture of my ancestors in my bones was calling me to notice a newness arriving. Every new moon is an opportunity. This one, in particular, is the one to start again with.

I walked to the edge of the gentle sloping hill and looked out at the tiny, twinkling lights of houses across the valley on the other side. I always wondered what it was like inside houses I knew I'd never visit. Beautiful furniture, soups cooking, people drawing, kissing, fighting. I sat on a flat rock and tasted the tequila, licking the salty rim after each sip. My eyes adjusted to the dark. Then, I smelled the smoke. She was sitting a few feet away, her legs crossed on the dusty ground, her eyes in my eyes, piercing through house lights reflected in her glasses, surging through the black edges of the frames as though they were right up in my face.

You told me to leave you in Virginia, I said.

She smiled.

How do I leave you behind? I said.

I stood up and turned to walk away. As I turned, she was in front of me. This time, right up in my face, the way vampires in movies move, legless, flying and floating.

Know what you don't want, in order to know what you do want, she said.

I stood looking at her. She blew smoke in my face. I wanted her gone but now without animosity. I wanted the memory of her close and I wanted to disappear without her.

I don't want to care, I said.

Then don't, she said.

Her eyes were full of water. Real sea salt water, slow tears that fell onto my feet, in between my toes, flooding and wrinkling my skin like a body soaked in a bath too long.

I'm not mad, I said.

I dropped my tequila glass. It fell against a stone causing a piece of it to break clean off. Salty tequila spilled onto my feet mixing with her tears. I put my hands on her face. She took off her glasses. All the eyes, four eyes all one thing, closed. Kissing. Breathing. Then hugging. Then laughing.

Remember this moment.

Remember.

Remember before it's gone, before she's gone even though she already left.

I picked up the shards of broken glass and walked back to the house. Jo was asleep when I arrived. I crawled into the futon, careful not to wake her. As I closed my eyes, she put her hand on my back and we breathed together.

The next morning, Jo drove me to the Amtrak station. She didn't ask where I was going or why, but she gave me a mixtape and told me to listen to it once the train started moving.

Someone I loved made it for me a long time ago, she said. But I no longer need it. It's meant to be passed on, moved forward.

Know what you don't want. Or what you no longer need.

Know where the end is.

I thanked her and we hugged and kissed and I knew I would never see her again but we didn't talk about it. We didn't talk about staying in touch although I knew we'd stay connected even if we forgot about each other. Because I didn't forget anyone. I just couldn't remember everyone all at once.

37.

I wouldn't be me without her. And there was so much of me that was not her. Attachment is not connection, but the line between the two is almost invisible. She was woven into the thin layers of skin around my fingertips. Her icy water blue eyes stayed imprinted behind my own eyes. The sound of her voice never dulled in my ears. I left her in Virginia, in New York, in New Mexico, all over Europe. The ghost of her, of my past, of a love I wasn't sure was love but was, it was it was, stayed see-through and pale. I thought of her without grasping, but remembering. Memory is the dividing line.

There would always be beginnings. Everything is a beginning in its own way. Endings are more intermittent. You don't know it's an end until it's behind you. But I knew I was inside of the end.

A letting go.

A purge.

A long, painful, beautiful, disgusting, heartbreaking, liberating goodbye.

As solitary as writing can be, it's impossible to finish a book alone.

Many thanks and deep appreciation to:

Everwood Farmstead and Write On Door County for beautiful, magical residency space. I wouldn't have finished this book without that time.

Miriam McNamara, who pushed me into word count discipline in those residency weeks, and spent hours with me reading out loud, listening, and processing chapter after chapter. Thank you thank you thank you.

Summer Stewart and everyone at Unsolicited Press for editing, talking, being easy to work with, and pushing my work forward.

Alissa Hattman for perfect edits and beautiful words.

Darci Schummer, Brittany Ackerman, and Elisabeth Workman for reading and thinking and sharing thoughts and feelings.

Thank you friends, acquaintances, unknown readers, and random social media people who buy my books and like and share my stories. Every kind of support is meaningful.

ABOUT THE AUTHOR

Raki is a first generation American, queer, Jewish writer. She is the author of *The Things You Left* and *The Memory House*, both Minnesota Book Award finalists. Her work has appeared in numerous publications and has been shortlisted and nominated for several other awards, including the Pushcart Prize for Fiction and the Pen Faulkner Award in Fiction. She lives in Minneapolis and teaches creative writing at The Minneapolis College of Art and Design.

ABOUT THE PRESS

Unsolicited Press is based out of Portland, Oregon and focuses on the works of the unsung and underrepresented. As a womxn-owned, all-volunteer small publisher that doesn't worry about profits as much as championing exceptional literature, we have the privilege of partnering with authors skirting the fringes of the lit world. We've worked with emerging and award-winning authors such as Amy Shimshon-Santo, Brook Bhagat, Elisa Carlsen, Tara Stillions Whitehead, and Robyn Leigh Lear.

Learn more at unsolicitedpress.com. Find us on Instagram, X, Facebook, Pinterest, Bsky, Threads, YouTube, and LinkedIn. Unsolicited Press also writes a snarky newsletter on Substack.

www.ingramcontent.com/pod-product-compliance
Lightning Source LLC
Chambersburg PA
CBHW030004010826
48973CB00009B/2660